The Tales of Fluke & Tash in

Robin Hood Adventure

MARK ELVY

Available from

www.ypdbooks.com
and
www.flukeandtash.com

© Mark Elvy, 2015

Published by Fluke & Tash Publishing

A CIP catalogue record for this book is available from the British Library.

ISBN 978-0-9934956-0-1

Book layout by Clare Brayshaw

Prepared and printed by:

York Publishing Services Ltd
64 Hallfield Road
Layerthorpe
York YO31 7ZQ

Tel: 01904 431213

Website: www.yps-publishing.co.uk

The Tales of Fluke & Tash ...

Robin Hood Adventure

HaPPy READING!

M. C. ___

Tash

Hanging on was easy, but steering was a problem. The flight had been bumpy but thankfully short, and as she came into land, Tash skidded across the landing, through the bedroom door, avoided the bed, and managed to manoeuvre the magic suitcase so it came to an abrupt, shuddering halt against the wardrobe, which just happened to be the suitcase's normal home when not being used for her forays and adventures.

As she climbed off the suitcase she felt soft comfortable carpet under her paws, when just a few minutes ago it had been warm sand from the Arabian Desert, and as much as Tash liked sand, sometimes it was nice to be home surrounded by all her creature comforts.

She patted the magic suitcase with affection.

'See you on our next adventure,' she murmured as she carefully stored the suitcase inside the wardrobe, nestled behind clothes and jackets that hadn't been worn in ages, and shut the door carefully, and not a second too soon as she heard Dad's car pulling up the driveway.

What Dad would have thought if he had come home to an empty house didn't bear thinking about. Cats were meant to sleep all day and greet their owners when they came home from work, not be off gallivanting around the world.

Hastily making her way out of the bedroom, she entered the second spare room, her own room, which doubled as Dad's games room, complete with computer, dartboard and table football. She jumped up onto the orange sofa, curled up as only a cat can, and pretended to be asleep. Footsteps made their way up the stairs and a face appeared in the doorway.

Dad came in and ruffled Tash's head.

'Asleep again then, Tash?' he said 'must be boring being a cat, sleeping all day.' As he made his way back onto the landing, one foot on the top step of the stairs, he stopped, looked down, and noticed small specks of sand on the carpet.

'Where's all this sand come from?' he muttered. 'It was weeks ago we came back from holiday, and I'm sure we vacuumed the carpet last night.' He shook his head as he made his way down the stairs.

'That was close,' thought Tash, inspecting her paws and licking away the residual sand that still remained. 'Must be more careful next time, can't have Dad finding out about my adventures.' She finished her mini cleansing session, and curled up for a proper sleep this time, drifting off, dreaming about her recent adventure with that brave Lieutenant Colonel, Lawrence of Arabia, in the desert helping the Arab army revolt against the dreadful Ottoman Empire.

The following day was Saturday, and both Mum and Dad were at home. Dad had been out in the garden most of the morning raking up leaves that had fallen from the trees, forming neat mounds of them dotted around the garden.

The pair of them had seemed different today, acting a bit strange, excited for some reason, and the excitement grew when the phone rang. Tash could hear snippets of conversation as Mum talked on the phone, and then she hollered to Dad.

'Come on, are you ready? They've said we can collect in a couple of hours!' and Dad trooped off back into the house.

Collect? Thought Tash, *must be talking about some shopping they need to get.* She forgot about the conversation as she eyed up the tempting piles of leaves.

Tash loved leaves – indeed adored them. She loved to play in them, dive in amongst them, and pretend to catch enemy mice or other such critters that dared to invade her garden. Well

Dad just about hit the roof when he came back out to put away his rake and lock up the shed. The garden, which just a few minutes ago had neat piles of leaves ready to be bagged up, now looked a mess. It looked for all the world as if a huge tornado had swept through, with leaves everywhere. Tash decided now would be a good time to sneak off, and headed back into the house.

She nipped in through the cat flap, which swung shut with a squeaking noise. *Must get those hinges oiled,* she thought, and made her way through the kitchen and up the steep stairs, which when you're tired always seemed like climbing Mount Everest, the biggest mountain in the world. She made a mental note to visit Everest one day and see how high it really was. Maybe she could help Sir Edmund Hillary be the first person to reach the summit – now that really would be cool, the thought of being the first cat to climb Everest was definitely worth considering.

She jumped up on to her comfy sofa and began to doze off, dreaming of leaves, mice and wondering where her next adventure would take her.

Fluke

Spots! Hundreds, if not thousands of them, were my first introduction to the world as I opened my eyes for the first time.

I was surrounded by them, mostly black spots, although some were brown. Later that first afternoon I was formerly introduced to my brothers and sisters, that was after the vet had given me the once over, stuck a couple of needles in me, *inoculations* the vet called them, apparently they were meant to stop me from catching any infections.

My stomach rumbled. I didn't know what it was at the time, though later I discovered they called it hunger. Apparently I was always hungry, so after I was re-introduced to my mum, lovely lady that she was, she cleaned me thoroughly, and after my first bath she fed me, and the stomach stopped rumbling.

The first few weeks were a bit of a blur. We played a lot, ate a lot, and even though I was last to be born, I was by far the biggest, and my smaller but elder brothers and sisters all seemed to look up to me. Apparently I was the ring leader; some have said since that I was also a trouble maker, but I preferred *mischievous* or *inquisitive*.

Different people arrived to check on our progress, and some jabbed more needles in us. *How many inoculations could there be?* I wondered.

We chewed anything that was chewable and some things that weren't, and our small teeth grew. I dare say we probably annoyed Mum a heck of a lot, as she was always telling us off.

Slowly we all started to grow; Mum's food gave us the required amount of nutrients, and I seemed to grow the fastest. I couldn't help being hungry all the time.

After several weeks, people used to say *doesn't he look like his dad?* Well my dad was lovely, but he wasn't the brightest candle in the box. Most of the time he used to lie in the garden chewing on a training shoe or someone's slipper and barking at anything that he thought needed barking at. I suppose I must have picked up some of his traits.

Over the coming days more visitors arrived and I noticed some of my brothers and sisters went off with them, until one day it was my turn.

I was introduced to a lovely couple, and my first action was to chew the man's shoe lace (I must have got that habit from my dad), and then

I stuck my head in the lady's handbag. I was just checking for needles as I didn't fancy any more inoculations, and, well, she did just leave it lying invitingly on the floor and I was inquisitive after all. Eventually I was scooped up, stroked and petted.

They called me *Fluke*, and so at last I had a name, an identity, I was someone other than just *spot, spotty* or *trouble maker* and as I looked over my shoulder at my few remaining brothers and sisters I wondered if I would ever see them again. My last view of my family was Mum in the garden and Dad chewing another slipper – fond memories indeed.

If I am honest, I was a little bit scared: this was a change from the norm, and as I sat on the lady's knees in the back of their car, I wondered what the future held. Did I really want to spend my days chewing slippers or was there more to learn? Tiredness took over and with a big yawn, I fell asleep. The lap was comfy and the driving was smooth.

The big surprise

What only seemed like minutes but was really three hours later Tash woke with a start. The family estate car pulled up the drive and doors were opened and slammed shut.

Oh they're back then, thought Tash as she jumped off the sofa, stretched, and started to make her way down the stairs of Mount Everest, ready to greet Mum and Dad. They had both rushed out of the door soon after the phone call so something must have been important.

Must have returned from the supermarket, thought Tash, hoping they had been shopping as she was starving and noticed the supply of cat food in the cupboard was getting very low. *I wonder what food and toys they've brought me today, hopefully a nice big tin of tuna and some tasty biscuits.* Her mouth started to water at the prospect of a fish supper.

Tash paused halfway down the stairs and sat on a step. The key rattled in the front door which was flung wide open.

'TASH' Mum shouted, 'we're home, where are you? 'We've got you a nice surprise.' Without any more warning Tash was greeted by a big spotty dog's head, a Dalmatian, well, a puppy to be exact, but still, quite a large if slightly tubby puppy. *Maybe that's where the term puppy fat comes from!*

They stared at each other for a moment then chaos exploded. Spotty dog saw Tash, got excited, and pulled the lead from Mum's grasp. Mum tripped over the step in her failed attempt to hang onto the lead.

'Fluke, noooooo!' shouted Dad, clambering over Mum sprawled on the floor. Fluke launched himself at Tash halfway up the stairs, his lead trailing behind him. He didn't know why he chased the cat; he didn't really even know what a cat was, but some instinct made him want to chase, and it felt like fun and Fluke liked fun.

Fluke tried to get at Tash behind Tash's sofa in the games room. Unfortunately for Fluke he was three times the size of the cat and got himself stuck, wedged between the sofa and the wall. He couldn't go forwards or backwards. The first thing dad noticed when he entered the room was Flukes spotty bum sticking out from behind the sofa. Tash saw her chance and jumped back over Fluke, scrambled along his spotty back, and fled back down the steep stairs of Everest, taking two or three steps at a time. Mum got unsteadily to her feet clutching an empty shopping bag, and was about to pick up the tins of dog food from the living room floor when Tash rocketed between her legs causing Mum to lose her balance, slip on one of the tins, and land unceremoniously in a heap, surrounded by more tins of the dog food.

Tash headed for the emergency exit, her cat flap in the utility room, nearly tearing it off its hinges in her bid for freedom and the safety of the back garden. She clambered up one of the trees in record time, secured herself in a cosy tree-house she had made, and settled in to look back over the garden towards the house.

What were they thinking? She thought, *bringing a dog into my house?* Well Mum and Dad paid the mortgage, so technically it was theirs.

How long was spotty going to be staying? Tash thought. From the number of dog food tins Tash had seen rolling round the floor it could be quite a long time.

Surely they haven't gone and bought themselves a dog? And where is he going to sleep? These questions rushed through Tash's head. *And no way, not in a million years, is he sleeping in MY bed!* She shuddered at the thought, as she continued to count off a list of questions on the claws of her paw.

So you're a cat then?

Over the rest of the day, Mum and Dad made several trips to and from the car, bringing in an assortment of items which consisted of dog leads and collars, of which there were several styles, some with studs on and some with flashing lights, a whole box of irritating squeaky toys, loads more food, and one item which really pleased Tash more than anything, a massive spotty bed. At least that sorted out the sleeping arrangements.

A few days passed and Tash had been mainly consigned to the garden, only venturing inside the house late at night when Fluke was taken upstairs to sleep in Mum and Dad's bedroom, who thought it best for the first few nights until he settled into his new home. The bedroom door had been kept firmly shut to stop him from trying to climb up or down the steep stairs.

Tash noticed, with some delight, from her vantage point in the tree house that Fluke hadn't really mastered the art of climbing stairs.

Taking a long run at it, occasionally he made it to the top step, but more often than not he only managed to get halfway up before he tumbled unceremoniously back down to land in a spotty heap at the foot of the stairs.

During the day, Tash's food had been left out for her in the normal place on the utility room floor, but had often been gobbled down by a greedy Fluke, who seemed to love the extra dinner provided, So Mum soon resorted to leaving Tash's food outside the cat flap on the patio. Alfresco dining, as grown-ups call it, is all the rage, but eating outside was OK as long as the weather was good.

At times Tash caught Fluke staring at her through the clear plastic window of the cat flap, watching in envy as she ate every last morsel, wondering why he couldn't be in the garden playing.

Tash was still a bit cautious about Fluke, mainly due to his size, but was beginning to realise he was sort of OK; he seemed harmless enough – a bit mad and boisterous, and he did seem to be getting into mischief all the time, which suited Tash as she loved adventure, and had been known to get into the odd scrape or two herself.

Tash made the decision. She couldn't keep up this alfresco dining any more, and didn't like being barred from her house except for late at night. Tonight she would be bold, make some introductions, and hope that her gut instincts about Fluke were correct.

So later that night, all was quite in the house: Mum and Dad were in bed sound asleep, and Fluke, who had now been allowed to sleep downstairs on his own, was apparently snoozing in his oversized bed.

Tash made her way as quietly and carefully through the cat flap as she could, although the hinges did squeak a little when the flap swung shut. Entering the darkened kitchen, the only light available was via the illuminated clocks on the oven and microwave. She peered round the door frame, and padded across the kitchen and looked into the dark living room. Her superb night vision adjusted quickly to the dark, and she spied Fluke's massive bed in the centre of the room. *Oh my God,* thought Tash, *how big is this dog going to get?*

All seemed in order; the house was quiet, except for Dad's snoring that could be heard halfway down the street. Taking extra care to keep the noise down, Tash skirted round the outside edge of the room, stopping every now and then to listen for any new sounds. She plucked up the courage and was about to tiptoe over to the oversized dog's bed, when suddenly she heard a sleepy voice from within.

'So you're a cat then? Not sure that I've ever met a cat before.' Tash thought she had been silent so plainly Fluke was no fool after all.

A startled Tash walked cautiously walked over to Fluke's bed, almost needing a step-ladder to peer over the edge, it was that big and made eye contact with Fluke.

'Yep that's me, the name's Tash, pleased to meet you,' and carefully she reached into the bed with an outstretched leg and both Fluke and Tash shook paws in a friendly greeting.

'So I'm guessing your name's Fluke?' purred Tash.

'How do you know my name? I only found out myself a few days ago,' queried Fluke.

'Well,' muttered Tash, 'it might have something to do with *Aahh isn't Fluke wonderful,* or *Isn't Fluke a real sweetie* or maybe it was *No Fluke, not the kitchen floor again, your toilet's outside* laughed Tash. 'That's all I've heard for several days now, Fluke this and Fluke that. Anyway, why aren't you trying to chase me?' continued Tash, 'or are you scared you might get stuck behind the sofa again?'

'Yeah sorry about that, I don't know what came over me, I just had the urge to chase something. Three hours in the back of that car and I just wanted to get out and stretch my legs,' Fluke said rather shyly.

'Don't worry about it, I was a bit startled I have to admit, but it was kind of fun, and also the size of you made me a bit wary, but now I've met you you're not as scary as I first thought.'

'Scary? I don't look scary do I?' said Fluke, slightly worried, desperate for a mirror to check on his reflection and see what he looked like.

'So where are you from?' said Tash, changing the subject, wanting to know a bit more about Fluke.

'Not sure really,' confirmed Fluke. 'One minute I'm with my mum, dad, brothers and sisters and before I realise it I've moved away and left them all behind. It's all new to me, different house, new garden and a new family.'

'Well, let me be the first to say it will be a pleasure having you around,' Tash said warmly. 'It gets a bit lonely at times being the only animal around the house,' she continued, 'now I've got someone to hang out with and share some adventures, and if we do get into mischief we can at least get into mischief together, double trouble eh?'

'Sounds good to me,' Fluke said with relief, 'I was beginning to think you didn't like me much, not having said hello. What sort of adventures?' he asked, ears pricked up in anticipation.

'Don't be silly, I was just being careful and wanted to get to know you a bit before I said hi, and as for adventures, well where do I begin?' Tash purred. 'Can't tell you tonight Fluke, I need to explain a few things first, let's get you settled in, then I'll explain a bit more,' she continued. 'All I'll say is don't make too many plans for tomorrow as I'll give you the official welcome tour; we'll wait until we've got the house to ourselves first mind you.'

They chatted a while longer and agreed it was time for a nap, Fluke wanted to be fresh for the morning's welcome tour.

'See you in the morning then Tash,' he yawned, rested his head on his paws and promptly fell fast asleep, with Tash making her way upstairs to her sofa, glad she had at last broken the ice and spoken to Fluke, and that they were at last on speaking terms.

The grand tour

Fluke was woken early the next morning by Dad stumbling down the stairs, hair all over the place, still half asleep, and moaning about having to go to work. He made himself a couple of rounds of toast and a huge pot of tea, whilst Mum appeared from upstairs and dished up a hearty breakfast for both Tash and a very eager Fluke who couldn't wait christen his new food bowl..

Mum looked over at Dad. 'Glad they're getting on at long last and Fluke's not chasing Tash anymore,' I thought we'd made a mistake bringing a dog into the house'

'Oh they're fine now,' agreed Dad, 'just took a bit of time that's all – and Tash can look after herself, and look at them together, best of buddies now, Fluke seems to have settled right in.' Mum and Dad stood quietly watching, both looking into the utility room at the pair eating breakfast. Satisfied, they turned back and made their way upstairs to continue getting ready for work.

'Crikey Fluke, your new bowl's the size of a bucket,' said Tash nibbling at the food in her small dainty dish.

Fluke however was the complete opposite. He could hardly hear what Tash was saying; his head was buried deep into his bowl, and he was eating so fast as if he'd not eaten in days. The bowl was moving round the kitchen floor like it had a mind of its own, Fluke desperately chasing it round the kitchen trying to make sure every last morsel was polished off. His breakfast finished in double quick time, his new bowl was licked so thoroughly clean it hardly needed to be put into the dishwasher. He then sat watching Tash nibble at her breakfast, hoping that she might leave him some.

Mum and Dad returned to the kitchen, both ready for work. Fluke was then encouraged to visit next door neighbour's fence for more toilet training before Dad locked the patio door. 'See you at lunchtime,' Dad muttered as he patted Fluke's head, and they headed out of the front door and off to work.

Mum was heard to whisper as they both left: 'Do you think they'll be OK alone for a few hours, it's the first time we've left them both together?'

'Of course they'll be OK,' Dad replied making his way out of the door, newspaper tucked under one arm, keys jangling in his hand, heading for his car. 'What possible mischief could they get up to in a few hours? Besides I'll be home for lunch to check up on them and let Fluke out into the garden.'

Once they had the house to themselves Tash turned tour guide and started the *Grand Tour*.

Starting upstairs in the second spare room, Tash began. 'This is our room and it doubles up as Dad's games room. Notice the computer terminal, table football and dartboard. This is the sofa, I believe you're familiar with it, especially how tight it fits to the wall' teased Tash. 'Now it's nice and comfy and large enough for both of us just as long as you don't take up too much room, and I always have the back edge of the sofa right under the window.'

Next room on the tour was Mum and Dad's master bedroom, and then another guest room, both nice enough but neither had a sofa to sleep on, so they both agreed their spare room was much better.

Trotting back downstairs, Tash showed Fluke where the spare key was kept, and taught Fluke how to open the patio door.

'You'll need to use the patio door Fluke, as I'm afraid if you try my cat flap, you'll either break it, get stuck, or probably both.'

They made their way into the back garden, with the sun shining brightly.

'Oh it's good to be outside,' said Fluke breathing in the fresh air. 'You're lucky having a private door to use,' he continued, meaning Tash's cat flap.

'If they had one for you it would probably take up most of the door,' said Tash jokingly.

Tash then started the *Grand External Tour,* which took them on a round trip of the garden, starting by the patio with its fine array of pot plants and garden furniture, and then making their way around the edge Tash showed Fluke all her camps, tree-houses and dens she had made over the years. The tour took a while due to the overall size of the garden and there was so much for Fluke to take in. She pointed out several trees and loads of bushes to play hide and seek behind.

Also on the tour Tash showed Fluke all the best sunbathing spots and her secret food stashes, just in case of emergencies like the supermarket shutting early, or the cat flap getting stuck – you could never be too careful

Last on the tour was an old tree stump. Fluke scratched his ear and was trying to make out what was so special about it – it must have some significance or else why would Tash bother to show him?

'OK, I give in, what's with the tree stump?' said Fluke. 'Is it a seat or just a garden ornament gone wrong?'

'This, my spotty friend,' Tash said pointing to the stump, 'is home to some very good friends of mine.'

'What, woodlice?' chuckled Fluke, enjoying his first joke of the day.

'No, not woodlice,' muttered Tash, shaking her head. 'Nummers,' she replied.

'Nummers?' said Fluke, what are Nummers?' Fluke clearly thought he had misheard.

'More like *who* are Nummers. They're a family of little people that live underground, a whole network of passages and tunnels spread all over the place. They're a type of elf, goblin or pixie. Adults don't remember them, children do when they're young, but soon forget when they get older, and not much is known about them. They're very small and live underground out of the way and are really friendly.'

'Wow,' said Fluke, clearly impressed. 'Tunnels eh? Wish I was small enough to visit them underground.'

Tash carried on. 'They use these tree stumps as doorways to their homes. Nobody knows they live here except me, and now obviously you, so keep quiet or the whole neighbourhood will be swarming with so-called experts, armed with spades and diggers, ripping up everything in sight in the name of scientific research!' Tash warned Fluke.

'Well I won't tell anyone,' said Fluke, 'but how do they get in or out?'

'Look more closely,' instructed Tash.

Fluke moved in closer, sniffed the base of the stump and watched in awe as a small concealed door opened, and out strode a family of Nummers, staring up at a dumbstruck Fluke. They were a greenish colour and blended in well with the surrounding vegetation. They had normal facial features although everything was a lot smaller, the main difference was what looked like a tube that came out of the side of their heads pointing upwards; it looked just like a snorkel that swimmers used for swimming under water.

'Fluke, meet the Nummers,' said Tash as she made the introductions.

Fluke crouched down to get a better view, and to say hello, 'I would shake your hands but I think my paws are a bit big,' he said leaning in close to listen for their reply.

'Pleased to meet you,' one of the Nummers said, and introduced himself as Stump. The Nummers were so tiny that Fluke had to listen really carefully as their voices was so quiet. 'So, you're Tash's new friend then?' questioned Stump. 'You'll probably see us around the garden if you look close enough, and we occasionally visit the house and pop in to see Tash when the humans are in bed or out for the day. Just be careful where you're walking with those big paws of yours as were that small you may miss us!'

The family of Nummers, Fluke and Tash carried on chatting for several more minutes until the conversation was interrupted by the sound of Dad's car coming down the street.

'Crikey is that the time? Quick Fluke, we better get you back inside and lock the door, before Dad gets in from work.'

Hasty farewells were exchanged and the Nummers turned round and disappeared through the little door in the base of the tree stump. The door shut firmly behind them and you wouldn't really know there was a door there unless you looked really carefully.

The pair managed to get the patio door locked and the key put back in its original place, and ran upstairs to the sofa.

Tash curled up one end and Fluke the other, both pretending to be asleep as they heard Dad climbing the stairs.

'That was a close shave,' whispered Tash and Fluke nodded in agreement.

Dad popped his head round the bedroom door and muttered: 'Well what a couple of lazy-bones you two are!' and went over to pat them both on the head. 'Had a nice first morning together then have we? Nice to see you've had a quiet morning and not been up to any mischief.'

Tash pretended to stretch and yawn. 'Who wants lunch then?' Dad shouted over his shoulder as he made his way back downstairs. Fluke didn't need to be asked twice and leapt of the sofa and bounded down the stairs in pursuit of Dad, nearly bowling him over like a tenpin in a bowling alley, such was his eagerness at the promise of more food.

The magic suitcase

The next few days followed much the same pattern. Mum and Dad went off to work in the morning, then either one or the other popped home at lunchtime, and both came home early evening, cooked dinner, and watched television, generally doing family things.

Fluke was introduced to a collar and lead for the second time, which he hated, and was constantly trying to do a Houdini escape act and release himself from the collar; but it was only put on when they went out for their morning or evening walks, so he could just about live with that.

They went over the park, around the lake and into the nearby woods, which meant that Fluke was re-introduced to the car, but now he was considered old enough to go in the back all by himself. He refused to lie down as there was too much to see, and being nosy he took in all the sights and sounds and stood all the way to the woods, occasionally sniffing the air through the open car window. At every tree stump they passed Fluke stopped, sniffed the stump and whispered *Hello* just in case any Nummers were at home, and on the odd occasion he spotted other families of Nummers he got a whispered *Morning!* in reply. Dad was completely oblivious and thought Fluke was just looking for food.

The days passed, and late one afternoon Tash whispered to Fluke: 'Right, Fluke, now it's time to introduce you to some serious adventuring. Just be ready tonight about midnight. Once Mum and Dad are asleep, meet me in the spare room, and be ready for a fun night out.'

'OK,' whispered Fluke, 'what are we doing at midnight?' who could hardly contain himself, he was getting that excited.

'Just wait, be patient and you'll see,' said Tash. 'I told you to expect some fun didn't I? Well tonight it starts!'

Bedtime came, and this time Fluke went upstairs with Mum and Dad and stretched out on the bedroom floor.

He kept staring at the digital clock, the soft red light casting a comforting glow around the room. Fluke was willing it to reach midnight and at exactly 12:02 he heard the cat flap open and close with that distinctive squeaking of the hinges.

Tash crept up the stairs muttering *these stairs get steeper every day,* who one day longed to live in a bungalow without stairs! She popped her head round the bedroom door and whispered to Fluke, 'Are you ready then?'

'I've been ready since this afternoon when you first told me,' said Fluke quietly.

'Come on then, follow me,' commanded Tash, who led the way across the landing, under the ironing board that seemed to live permanently in an upright position, and was never folded up and put neatly away.

They both crept into the spare room and Tash headed for the wardrobe on the back wall. Opening the door with a bit of a struggle, she rummaged deep into the rear of the wardrobe and eventually dragged out an old, dusty suitcase and stood back to let Fluke admire it.

'Is that it?' moaned Fluke in a disappointed voice. 'This is what I've been waiting for all afternoon is it? An ancient looking, dust gathering suitcase that looks like it went out of fashion years ago, if it was ever in fashion in the first place!'

'Looks can be very deceptive Fluke. This isn't just any old suitcase, believe me, it's a very special suitcase. Yes you're right, it's old, it's battered and has travelled thousands of miles, but that's part of the secret, gathering magic dust everywhere it's been.'

'Magic dust?' said Fluke a bit warily. 'How does that work then, and what's magic about it?'

'I don't know how it works,' admitted Tash, 'or even why it works, and I don't really care, but trust me it just does work.'

'I still don't get what's magic about it?' said a confused Fluke, scratching an itchy spot behind his ear.

'Fluke let me introduce you to the time travelling, space hopping suitcase. We can travel anywhere in the world and back to any time in history on this old suitcase!'

'Wow!' exclaimed Fluke clearly in shock, 'are you pulling my paws? You mean I can go back in time and eat my breakfast again and again and again ?'

'Trust you Fluke, no wonder you're tubby. I've got a feeling this is going to be a very long night!'

Bows, arrows and green tights

'So what happens now then?' said Fluke cautiously, still not totally convinced this wasn't one big wind up at his expense.

'Well, notice the round dials or wheels on top of the suitcase each side of the handle? They're numbered 0,1,2,3,4,5,6,7,8,9.' Tash was pointing to the dials as she was instructing Fluke. 'These little wheels on a normal suitcase are for the combination locks. There are four little wheels on one side of the handle, and an identical set of four wheels the other side of the handle. Do you understand so far?'

Fluke nodded and Tash carried on explaining. 'One set of numbered wheels is used to set the date and time in history, and the other set is used as place co-ordinates, a bit like a road map. There was this old book inside the lining of the case giving detailed instructions and more importantly co-ordinates to every time and place in history, so don't lose the book or we won't be going anywhere!'

'OK, now what?' panted Fluke, getting more and more excited.

'Firstly open the case and put your paw into the zip compartment.' Fluke did as he was told which he never did when Mum and Dad asked him anything.

'What can you feel inside?' asked Tash.

'I don't know, feels like clothes of some sort.' Reaching deeper into the zip compartment Fluke pulled out a whole new outfit, the colour of Lincoln green; next out came a bow and arrow set, the kind used at medieval archery contests; then followed a long wooden quarterstaff, a type of pole for close combat fighting; and finally a green hat complete with feather in the rim.

Tash then helped herself to a costume, exactly the same but on a smaller scale. Quickly putting on the outfits they studied each other and burst out laughing. Fluke had the bow and bag of arrows slung over his shoulder, and the long quarterstaff strapped to his back.

'What do you look like?' laughed Tash.

'Well you don't look any better,' smirked Fluke, struggling to get the green tights to fit properly.

Tash continued to explain. 'The magic suitcase automatically picks a costume relevant to the date in history and the place co-ordinates. I'd already decided on a time for us, and as it's your first adventure I wanted to go somewhere really cool and I don't mean the North Pole!'

Tash knew where they were going would be exciting but it could also be very dangerous. The date in history was set as 1194, the place medieval England. The co-ordinates were set for Sherwood Forest, the home of Robin Hood.

Hold on Tight

'What happens now, do we climb inside?' said Fluke.

'Don't be silly,' said Tash shaking her head in disbelief, 'what happens if you get locked in? How will you get out again? NEVER ever climb inside a suitcase, it's very dangerous. You sit on top like a bicycle, set the co-ordinates, close your eyes, keep your paws crossed and twist the handle three times.'

Both Fluke and Tash jumped on board the suitcase, Tash double checked she had set the co-ordinates correctly then said: 'Hold on tight, here we go, ready for take-off!'

'Wait a minute!' shouted Fluke as he climbed off and bent down to look under the bed, 'I've dropped my lunch and treats,' he whined as he scrambled under the bed to find his missing lunchbox. Climbing back on the case, lunchbox carefully hidden inside his green tunic, Fluke was ready to continue.

Tash eyed him with a look that was obvious she wasn't impressed. 'Food again? Are you sure you're ready this time? You've not forgotten anything else like your supper, midnight feast, breakfast, toothbrush, overnight bag, or bed? And why have you brought enough food to feed a whole family?'

'Thought we might have a picnic when we get there,' muttered Fluke.

'Hold on tight,' instructed Tash, 'this could be a bumpy ride.' Fluke took one last look around the room, noticed the digital clock was showing a time of 12:22, he then closed his eyes and held on tight. Tash turned the handle three times. Fluke thought he could feel the room spinning; he could hear the wind pick up which caused his ears to start flapping behind him.

'I'm getting dizzy,' shouted Fluke above the noise of the wind. 'What's happening?'

'We have take-off,' laughed Tash who was enjoying herself. 'Don't panic Fluke, it always feels weird on your first flight, just don't look down.'

Well, when Fluke was told to do something he normally did the opposite, so he opened his eyes and looked over the edge of the suitcase, immediately wishing he had listened to Tash. The ground looked a million miles away, and Fluke wasn't sure if he liked heights.

Loads of fluffy white clouds below, it looked just like a great big white woolly carpet. He quickly closed his eyes again and muttered in Tash's ear: 'How long to go before we land?'

'Seconds Fluke, only takes a few seconds, the flight doesn't take long, nearly there now, get ready for a bumpy landing!'

'Bumpy landing?' exclaimed a startled Fluke.

'In all these years I still can't steer or land it properly!'

There was an almighty crash as the suitcase drove straight through some bushes, hopped, skipped and jumped over a stream just like a flat stone being skimmed over water, and finally came to rest against the massive trunk of a very large oak tree.

'You can open your eyes now Fluke,' said Tash eager to see the look on Fluke's face. Fluke this time did as he was instructed, gradually peeking all around, eyes now wide open like saucers.

'It works Tash, it really works!' gasped Fluke climbing off the case, taking in his new surroundings, listening to the sounds of the forest, birds tweeting, rustling noises coming from the bushes all round as small animals that had been disturbed by the flying suitcase were now settling back down to whatever small animals in bushes did during the day. 'So where are we again?' carried on a gob-smacked Fluke.

'Sherwood Forest near Nottingham, and it looks like we're deep in the heart of the woods. Come on Fluke, pack up your things, grab our provisions and supplies and let's go for a walk and see what adventures we can find.'

'What's so special about Sherwood Forest then?' Fluke asked.

'I love reading about history,' Tash replied, 'and Sherwood Forest is the home of Robin Hood, a famous character who lived in the woods along with all his friends. They called all his followers the merry men and they would do anything to help their master Robin. They were into mischief and adventure themselves, battling against the evil Sheriff of Nottingham who was always trying to capture Robin. The Sheriff labelled them all as outlaws, but Robin was really one of the good guys; he and his men used to stand up to the evil Sheriff and try to put right all the evil things the Sheriff and his cronies did to the local people.'

Tash made sure the suitcase was well hidden, and made a mental note of their position so they could easily find it when they needed to return home.

They both agreed this was much better than sleeping, and made sure their bows, arrows and quarterstaffs were fixed comfortably over their shoulders and then headed off deeper into the forest.

Fluke couldn't wait any longer and started to rummage through his lunchbox for a snack, and had to run to keep up with Tash who was striding purposefully into the woods.

'Hope you're not dropping litter on the floor,' said Tash. 'Mind you we could follow the trail of dog biscuit wrappers back to the suitcase so at least we wouldn't get lost,' she chortled to herself.

Fluke noticed their costumes blended in with the surrounding shrubs, trees and bushes, and on a few occasions when he looked up from his snacking he almost lost sight of Tash between the foliage.

I can't swim

Fluke was looking all round in complete awe; he had never realised the outside could be so big, with trees as far as the eye could see in all directions.

'We'll never go short of toilets out here will we Tash,' said Fluke suddenly as he remembered his first day's puppy toilet training. No fences, but plenty of trees and not one carpet or kitchen floor.

'Sherwood Forest, home to Robin Hood, an outlaw that stole from the rich and gave to the poor,' said Tash as she started to educate Fluke a bit further.

'You keep saying outlaw?' said Fluke, 'I always thought they were bad people?'

'Some were, yes, but Robin Hood was one of the good guys, a real hero, besides you haven't got any money to steal so what are you worried about!' continued Tash stepping over a tree root.

Unfortunately for Fluke he looked up from his snacking a bit too late, got his paw hooked under the tree root and took an almighty tumble, spotty head over spotty bum as he carried on rolling down a steep moss covered mound, coming to rest at the edge of a wide river.

Fluke picked himself up, trying to adjust his green tights which kept slipping down and blew away a leaf that had worked its way into the corner of his mouth.

'Keep your mouth closed next time you fall into a pile of leaves,' said an envious Tash who just loved leaves and there were millions of them all over the place. 'Mum and Dad would be here for years tidying this lot up!'

Fluke's green tights slipped down again, so Tash stripped some bark off a fallen tree and made a belt for Fluke's ever expanding waistline.

'There you go, tie this round your waist, it will help to keep your tights up.'

'Well that was lucky,' said Fluke staring at the long, wide and very wet river that seemed to disappear miles into the distance, to both their left and right.

'I can't swim and I nearly went in head first!'

'I'm sure you could have used your sandwich box as a life raft,' tittered Tash, always ready to crack a joke at Fluke's expense.

'Well, now what do we do?' exclaimed Fluke, looking nervously at the large gap between the river banks, 'I don't like water!'

'It's obvious,' said Tash, 'we'll walk down the riverbank until we can find a way across.'

Heading left, they wandered off in search of an easier crossing, Fluke trailing behind slightly: but after his recent tumble down the mound he kept his eyes firmly open and looked intently to the ground. *No more embarrassing tumbles for me*, he thought to himself.

The sun was shining through the overhead canopy of trees, birds were singing in the treetops, and without realising Tash found herself whistling away to the tune *Robin Hood, Robin Hood, riding through the glen* Fluke decided to sing the verses but was completely out of tune, though as he pointed out there was nobody around to listen anyway.

After five minutes Fluke stopped his singing and whispered, 'I think we're being followed.'

Tash tried to impersonate an owl and swivelled her head as far as it would go. When eventually she had turned a complete circle, but couldn't see anything, she turned to Fluke. 'Where?' she whispered back.

'There, on the other side of the riverbank.' Fluke pointed in the general direction where he thought he had heard some noise. 'It sounded like twigs snapping under the weight of heavy footsteps, oh I do hope it's not that outlaw Robin come to rob me of my lunch,' wailed Fluke.

'He's probably come to shut your singing up,' stated Tash, 'your dodgy tuneless singing has probably alerted everybody in a five mile radius where we are and they've all come to find out who's making such a row!'

Three's a crowd

They stood still for a whole ten minutes, barely saying a word. No more noises were heard and they didn't see any movement in the trees and bushes opposite on the far bank, so they carried on in search of a suitable crossing point.

Shortly they came across a large fallen tree, which thankfully for them had fallen across a narrower stretch of the river, providing a makeshift bridge.

'You first then,' said Fluke, 'or better still can you carry me across?' he asked hopefully.

'What, a big heavy lump like you? I can't carry you, your equipment and your lunchbox. You're way too heavy, besides it's only a bit of water.'

'I've never had swimming lessons and it looks deep, plus my new outfit will get all soaking wet and be ruined,' whined Fluke.

'Well you better not fall in then had you, just follow what I do and use your quarterstaff to balance yourself, just like at the circus with the trapeze artist on the high wire.'

Tash put one paw on the tree trunk with her quarterstaff held out to keep her balance and started off across the trunk, eyes down watching her own footsteps carefully. She got nearly halfway across when she suddenly stopped, causing Fluke to bump into her, nearly tipping both of them into the water.

Fluke wheeled his legs and paws around in the air, desperately trying to keep both his balance and his dignity.

Regaining her composure she looked up and noticed the bushes rustling on the far bank.

She saw a very large man with a big bushy beard, dressed like them in a similar costume of Lincoln green, who had started to make his way across the tree trunk towards them.

Fluke hadn't noticed the stranger and complained to Tash: 'Why have we stopped? And please give me some notice next time will you! Come on, keep moving, we're nearly there!' He gazed nervously at the water streaming under the tree, seeing visions of himself floundering in the river and being carried off downstream.

Tash pointed to the stranger. 'THAT'S why! Have you seen the size of him, he's enormous, we'll never be able to pass each other, there's definitely no room for the three of us on this log.'

Meeting in the middle the tall stranger said in a deep booming voice: 'So what do we have here then? A dog and cat on a log and in my way! I'm in a hurry, so out of my way you two, step aside now and let me pass!'

'I can't turn round,' wailed Fluke clinging hold of Tash's green tunic, 'I'm going to fall in, can't you ask him to move backwards?' pleaded Fluke.

'You ask him if you want him to step back!' exclaimed Tash as she nipped through Fluke's legs and shoved him closer to the giant who blocked their way.

'We were on the bridge before you, so why can't you turn round and let us cross first? And, err, if it helps, I'll even say please!' said Fluke a bit more bravely than he actually felt.

The duel

The stranger's booming laugh echoed through the forest. 'Well aren't you two something, you're not from these parts are you? You obviously don't know who I am, because if you did you would be running away with your tails between your legs!

'So what will it be? A nice wet soak in the river or move out of my way and let me pass?' carried on the big man who stood on the tree trunk with arms folded waiting for their reply.

Tash returned through Fluke's shaking legs and fronted up to the large stranger.

'Look kind sir, we mean you no trouble, but my friend here can't swim – and yes we are new to your lovely forest, but we can't go backwards for fear of falling in, and to be honest as my friend said we were here first.'

'You leave me no option then,' laughed the stranger. 'Looks like I'm going to have to teach you two a lesson you'll never forget. We shall fight a duel! Whoever wins passes safely to the opposite riverbank, and who ever loses goes for a swim.'

'Duel? Did he really challenge us to a duel? Please tell me we're not fighting this giant?' said Fluke, legs and knees shaking so much now he was struggling to stand.

The stranger, who Tash thought looked very familiar, drew out his quarterstaff and made ready to do battle. His weapon of choice was an enormous length of sturdy looking wood. Worn and well-used, it fitted the giant's huge hands like it was made to measure. It also had the look of a weapon that had seen a lot of action!

Tash prepared herself, just like Obi-Wan Kenobi the Jedi Master (she'd watched *Star Wars* hundreds of times!), but using her quarterstaff instead of a light sabre she leapt at her opponent, staff swirling above her head, cutting through the air with loud swishing noises, and then the staffs clashed together and she nearly tumbled into the river below; the stranger's obvious strength was already causing big problems.

Tash managed to whack him on the shins a couple times and poke him in the stomach, and then had to dart out of the way before he could retaliate.

The main advantage she had was speed and agility. They traded a couple more blows which nearly sent Tash spinning into the water and she realised very quickly she couldn't carry on much longer as he was way too strong.

However she was cunning; knowing she couldn't win by strength alone, she somersaulted in mid-air and landed behind her attacker, and as he turned his head to find his elusive sparring partner it was Fluke's turn to enter the fray and have a go.

Well, considering this was Fluke's first time on a log, first time anywhere really, Tash wasn't expecting too much, and unfortunately she was right.

He took one almighty swipe with his quarterstaff, like a massive golf swing, missed his target completely, and considering his target was the size of a large house that was saying something, lost his balance and started to fall towards the water below.

Fortunately for Fluke his reactions were quick: he managed to grab hold of the green shirt of the stranger with one paw and hold onto his quarterstaff with the other.

Holding on for dear life they were both hanging over the edge of the trunk, looking down Fluke could see his terrified reflection in the water below.

As they both struggled to stay on the log, a large dog bone fell out of Fluke's lunchbox hidden in his tunic. The stranger lost his footing as he slipped on the dog treat. At the same moment, sensing victory, Tash leapt from behind and landed on the stranger's back, her paws round his head covering his eyes so he couldn't see where to put his feet.

Blindfolded by Tash, the giant placed one foot over the edge of the log and Fluke neatly used his quarterstaff to help propel him over the edge by shoving him in the back.

Tash leapt back on the log and grinned at Fluke, and as a huge splash erupted from the river below they both shouted. 'Enjoy your swim!' and 'Loser, loser', they chanted in unison, giving each other high fives.

The stranger stood waist deep, which to any normal person would be shoulder high, glaring at his two victors standing proudly on the log, and not quite understanding how he had been beaten by a cat and dog.

'Come on Fluke, leg it quick before the jolly green giant gets the right hump and chases after us!' Fluke didn't need to be told twice, and for once he obeyed an order.

Picking up his dog bone he shoved it back inside the lunchbox which was then tucked neatly back inside his tunic, and followed Tash along the rest of the log and they both disappeared into the thick green forest.

Time for a breather

They ran for what seemed like ages, eventually coming up to a wooded glade. They stopped and rested against a large oak tree to catch their breath.

'I'm shattered,' panted Fluke, tongue hanging out of the corner of his mouth in a bid to cool down.

'Oh you're just unfit,' said Tash, but in truth she was feeling tired herself.

'Let's rest here a while, it's a lovely sunny glade, with plenty of logs to sit on,' said Fluke.

Tash heartily agreed and they both sat on the nearest log and put their paws up to rest awhile.

'Well what an adventure so far,' said Fluke, 'you should have seen the look on the big guy's face when he went in the river!' Fluke chuckled.

'Well I've been thinking,' said a serious-looking Tash. 'Do you realise who we've just sent plunging into the river for an early evening bath? If I'm not mistaken it was Little John, one of Robin Hood's merry men, and he didn't look very merry or best pleased with us, so from now on we tread very carefully and watch our backs.'

'He'll never find us in this massive forest!' said Fluke a little nervously, spinning his head round to look in all directions.

'Oh I wouldn't be too sure about that,' stated Tash. 'This is, after all, Robin Hood's back garden and only the brave or foolish generally come through here uninvited without being robbed of all their money and treasure.' said Tash who was also constantly scanning the horizon and looking over Fluke's shoulder in the direction they had just come from.

Fluke meanwhile sat still, listening in awe, eyes open wide again like saucers as he took in all this information.

'Even the Sheriff won't dare come through here unless he's got his army of soldiers with him,' Tash carried on the storytelling.

'Who's this Sheriff fella then?' asked Fluke nibbling on a treat.

'He's the evil Sheriff of Nottingham, and is in charge of seizing an outlaw's property,' said Tash. 'He's employed by the King of England to look after the county of Nottinghamshire and the neighbouring county of Derbyshire. One of the Sheriff's jobs is to capture outlaws such as Robin Hood and to ensure the safety of trade routes through the Forest,' Tash continued and looked around once again to make sure they hadn't been followed.

'What's a trade route?' Fluke looked confused.

'It's like a main road, linking Nottingham to other towns. Don't forget they didn't have motorways like we're used to in our modern times. Back in the medieval era they were mainly single rough tracks, not tarmac as that hadn't been invented yet. These tracks wound their way through these forests and linked up all the major towns to each other. Tradesmen used these paths or tracks to take all their belongings and produce to the various markets dotted round the country.

'Oh I see, so this could be a busy route then? Maybe where we're standing now, could in the future, be a main road or even a motorway then?'

'Spot on! Err, sorry, no pun intended about spots,' said Tash and continued. 'The Sheriff's also meant to stop any outlaws from poaching the King's deer and venison which roam freely through these forests. They're the King's property and no one is allowed to poach.'

'So why is he so evil?' queried Fluke

'I read about him in history books. The Sheriff and his henchmen collect taxes from the people to pay the King. The Sheriff isn't paid an annual wage by the King. Instead, he has to pay a yearly sum of money to the King for the privilege of holding the lucrative title of Sheriff. Any money left over after he's paid the King is then the Sheriff's to keep, and believe me, he makes more than enough money from his various duties to pay the King and still make a handsome profit for himself as he is always scheming and coming up with new ways to tax the people and put more money in his own pocket!'

'And they called Robin an outlaw?' said Fluke. 'This Sheriff sounds a right handful!'

The storytelling continued for a while longer, and as the sun began to set, the heat of the afternoon sun all but disappeared, replaced with a chill in the air, causing both Fluke and Tash to shiver, although Tash suspected Fluke's shivering wasn't just the cold, but the thought of spending the night in a strange dark wooded forest with outlaws hiding in the trees.

The picnic

'Well it's beginning to get dark, we might as well stay here for the night,' said Tash, making a decision. 'Why don't you see if you can find some wood for the campfire, and I'll see about finding something to make a shelter. I suggest we build camp here and try to keep warm for the night.'

Fluke trudged off deeper into the woods, whistling bravely, not wishing to go too far on his own, just in case he got lost. Tash meanwhile busied herself gathering foliage, bracken and tree branches and started to construct a makeshift shelter, but after half an hour or so was starting to get slightly worried as she hadn't seen or heard Fluke for some time. She remembered hearing the out of tune whistling getting fainter as Fluke got farther away from camp but now she couldn't hear a thing, and as the shelter was finished she decided to see where her spotty friend had got to and what trouble he had found.

As Tash left the comfort of their camp she entered the outer fringes of the forest and followed a small path that wound its way into the forest.

'This must be the path that Fluke took,' she muttered to herself. 'Where can he be?' Suddenly she came upon Fluke staggering towards her dragging what looked like a big picnic hamper, full to the brim with food of all kinds, breads, cheeses, cold cuts of meat and what looked like small caskets of beer.

'Fluke, where have you been?' and gazing at the treasure trove of food she said 'and where on earth have you got all that food from?' Her gaze was searching the surrounding forest in the hope of seeing a big neon sign that flashed *Supermarket* although Tash was pretty certain they didn't have supermarkets back in the twelfth century.

'I found it in that clearing over there,' said Fluke proudly, a big grin spread over his face, pointing over his shoulder with his paw to indicate the general direction. 'It was just sat there on the floor in another clearing.'

'Show me where exactly,' said Tash, wondering off, Fluke trailing behind munching on some bread and cheese.

They both entered the clearing and sure enough there was left-over food and signs that someone had been here earlier. Tash skirted the outside perimeter of the clearing and stopped short as a loud noise came from the undergrowth, a noise that was repeated over and over again, a noise very familiar to Tash, the sound of loud snoring, just like Dad did at home keeping everybody awake. Someone was in a very deep sleep indeed.

Tash beckoned with her paw for Fluke to come over, and they both stood staring down at the portly figure dead to the world on the forest floor, snoring and mumbling in his sleep.

'That food you've just dragged back must belong to him,' said Tash, pointing to the overweight man, 'he might not take too kindly to us just helping ourselves,' she added.

'What, all that food for just one person?' queried Fluke. 'Mind you, he looks like he's got quite an appetite!' Fluke continued between mouthfuls of bread and cheese.

'Oh, and I suppose you wouldn't sit and polish it all off given half a chance?' said Tash grinning at Fluke.

'Well,' said Fluke, 'what do we do now? It seems such a waste to leave it, we may as well take it back to our camp, and he's not going to miss just a little bit of food is he? You said yourself we do need provisions after all!' exclaimed Fluke happily.

It was agreed, and they tiptoed away trying not to wake the sleeping stranger. Getting into trouble twice in one day was not something they really wanted to do.

Firewood was collected, many trips to and from camp were required both struggling with paws full of wood and kindling, Tash remembered how to start a campfire by whittling together two dry sticks and adding some kindling, then gently blowing on the glowing embers until the fire took hold, and gradually adding the wood. It was hard work, but worth it once the fire was going. There was something special about a good campfire and good food, and they sat round warming themselves, chattering away with stories about their adventure so far.

The pair of them polished off most of the picnic hamper they had rescued from the clearing earlier, and despite Tash's earlier misgivings about taking food she was glad they did as she had been starving. The only thing missing was a nice cup of tea: and Fluke loved his tea.

Both Fluke and Tash were warm and cosy. The heat of the campfire had warmed them through, and along with the snap, crackle and pop sound effects of the burning embers from the fire, and combined with full bellies, they both eventually began to feel drowsy.

Fluke couldn't keep his eyes open any longer and wanted his bed, so they both made their way towards their shelter after first hanging up their costumes on some hangers that Fluke had made earlier.

The shelter was quite basic, but at this present time neither could care less, and as soon as their heads touched the pillows of bracken and foliage, they were asleep, both snoring like the stranger they had stumbled across earlier.

Trip wire, what trip wiraaahhhh?

It was early and the forest was beginning to wake up. The sun had risen and sunlight was penetrating between the trees and branches. Last night's campfire was nearly out, with only a few small burning embers remaining.

Tash was awake and rubbing sleep out of her eyes when a shadow fell across the opening of the shelter.

'Wake up you two,' boomed a loud voice. 'I know there's two of you in there because I've seen the clothes hanging outside the entrance.'

Why does everybody round here have deep booming voices, thought Tash.

'And I assume looking at the left-over food around the campfire it was you two who stole my food last night?' the gruff voice outside the tent questioned to the now awake, if not fully alert, occupants of the makeshift shelter.

Tash nudged Fluke in the ribs, 'Fluke, why couldn't you have just left the food last night' whispered Tash urgently, 'you better get out there and explain.'

'Come out the pair of you. I can hear you whispering,' said the stranger again. 'Not answering is only going to make things worse for you both.' again the stranger tried unsuccessfully to get an answer from the two campers.

Fluke needed to leave the tent anyway as he was in need of the toilet, more so now he realised he was in trouble again! He was desperately trying to make an exit through the rear of the shelter rather than leave via the front where an angry stranger waited for them both.

As neither replied to the questions being directed at them, the stranger reached in and grabbed Fluke's tail, dragging him out. It was comical really, deep marks forming a groove in the dirt left by Fluke's claws and chin as he was dragged out unceremoniously from the tent, and was closely followed by Tash who strolled out of her own accord.

'Good morning kind sir,' said Tash greeting the stranger, 'and another fine day as well by the looks of it. It's going to be a warm day if I'm not mistaken.'

'Baking hot more like,' said the stranger. There were beads of sweat on his forehead as he cast his eye over Fluke and Tash.

'So what's a dog and cat doing camping in this part of the woods may I ask? And more importantly what have you got to say about stealing my food? Do you realise stealing is a serious crime?'

Fluke started to wail an apology explaining that last night they were hungry and promised not to do anything like that again, and begged the stranger not to lock them both up.

'Calm down spotty,' laughed the stranger, 'I'm not going to lock you up or report you, but I am going to insist you give me a hand to carry my belongings along this trail, because as your little friend said it is going to be a hot day and I'm sure you wouldn't want me to struggle in this heat all by myself would you now?'

They swapped names with each other; and as Tash had already guessed, the stranger was Friar Tuck.

Fluke and Tash got dressed in a hurry, the campfire was put out, and all their belongings were packed neatly away, leaving no mess lying around at all.

Fluke, being the strongest, was given some of the largest bags to carry and was soon wheezing away, sweat pouring down his face. 'Mr Tuck,' panted Fluke desperately trying to keep up, 'how much further are we going?'

'Not much further, Fluke,' confirmed the Friar, 'just on my way to visit some friends.' as Tash and Friar Tuck carried on walking and talking down some windy paths.

Tash was explaining to the Friar what they were doing here in the forest and the adventures they hoped to have, leaving their new companion very impressed, especially when he learnt of their duel on the log.

Fluke took the opportunity to take a short cut through the woods and came out a few yards ahead of the two chatterboxes, and was so happy with himself he failed to notice a vine rope crossing the track, covered in leaves and hidden carefully from view. The vine that crossed the track they were walking down eventually wound its way up the trunk of a very large oak tree next to them on the side of the track, and disappeared up into the canopy of leaves way above their heads.

Tash, being an expert on leaves, noticed too late that these leaves were positioned there on purpose and had not fallen naturally from the tree. She ran her eyes along the track, followed the vine up the tree trunk and realised with horror what was about to happen.

'Fluke,' she yelled, 'mind the trip wire!' Fluke, still happy that he was in front, turned to face Tash.

'Trip wire, what trip wiraaahhhh ?'

Too late! Both Fluke and Tash were whipped up off their paws with such force it took their breath away. They were catapulted upwards towards the tree canopy, suspended in a type of net that had been carefully hidden from view by the leaves, and were left hanging several feet above the forest floor looking down at Friar Tuck who was now laughing his head off.

'Pays to be careful and slow round these parts my friends,' he chortled. 'If I had been as careless as you two, I would also be hanging upside down looking silly!'

The sound of a distant bugle horn rang through the forest, and another horn seemed to answer it, this second one sounding close by.

Fluke tried to stand up in the net but that made things worse. Both paws slipped through holes in the base of the net and got stuck, his tail was caught up behind him, and his bow and arrows were also stuck fast. To complicate things, the more he struggled to free himself the more the net started to swing wildly out of control, spinning and swaying around so much Fluke wailed: 'I feel sick!'

'Will you stay still!' commanded Tash now trying to take control of the situation. 'You're making things worse, just don't move, let's think this through.'

Several seconds passed with only the sounds of creaking tree branches and a laughing Friar Tuck beneath them.

'Good start to the adventure,' muttered Tash. 'First we trespass through Robin Hood's garden evading outlaws and a dodgy Sheriff, then we send the biggest man I've ever seen in for a swim fully clothed, and if that's not enough, we steal a hamper full of food, and now to cap it all we're suspended from a very large oak tree with little hope of getting down. It really couldn't get much worse!'

So we meet again

'Er Tash,' whispered Fluke, 'I think it has just got worse, a whole lot worse! Take a look down and please let me know I'm dreaming.'

Tash did as she was instructed and saw that a large crowd had gathered under the suspended net. They had crept up very quietly and were in deep discussions with the Friar, immediately Tash knew what Fluke had meant.

Standing head and shoulders above everybody was the giant man from yesterday, Little John, but thankfully he now looked to have dried out.

Their eyes met and a rip-roaring belly laugh filled the forest.

'Well, well, what do we have here? Are my eyes deceiving me? It's my two little sparring partners from yesterday! My spotty friend and his companion the cat who fights like a tiger,' said Little John with a huge grin spread across his face. 'So we meet again eh? And guess what? There's only one way down,' laughed Little John.

Turning to look at his companions he bellowed, 'What do you think, Master Robin?'

'Well, I can't see a ladder,' laughed Robin Hood, unslinging his bow from his shoulder, pulling an arrow from his quiver, placing it into his bow string, and pulling back the taut string until the bow was stretched to its limit.

'He's going to shoot us!' blabbered Fluke, Tash was unsure, but thought she knew what was coming next. 'Hold on Fluke, I think we're going for another trip, downwards this time instead of up. Hang on to the rope!'

Robin Hood, expert archer, swordsman and all round hero took careful aim and let fly with his arrow. Both Fluke and Tash heard the arrow whistle past their ears and thud into the rope that was holding up the net, splitting it completely.

Gravity took over and the net plunged downwards to the ground quicker than it had gone up. Fluke's ears stood up vertically as the ground rushed up to meet them. Thankfully the bed of leaves on the forest floor cushioned most of the fall and they were both quickly free of the net, rolling around in the leaves, which got the better of Tash as for a second Tash thought she was back home in her garden chasing mice.

'Robin Hood I presume?' said Tash, composing herself whilst giving her clothes a brush down, paw outstretched to shake Robin by the hand. 'It's a pleasure to meet you at last and good shooting kind sir!'

Fluke had not been quite so lucky. He was stuck head first in a big mound of leaves, just his spotty bum was sticking up in the air, back legs kicking as he tried to turn himself the right way round.

'Here Fluke, let me help,' laughed the Friar, 'and let me introduce you to my friends, the friends I told you about earlier.'

Fluke tried to say thanks, but had a mouth full of leaves and was desperately trying to spit them out before he swallowed one: he may be always hungry but a feast of leaves and moss wasn't what he had in mind for lunch.

Again he had to hoist up his green tights that had managed to slip down his waist, tightening the belt that Tash had made him earlier.

The pair where introduced to the large group of merry men gathered round Robin, and Tash noticed they were nearly all wearing the famous Lincoln green costumes that both Fluke and Tash were wearing.

Amongst the group were Robin's cousin Will Scarlet, Much the Miller's son, Alan-a-Dale and David of Doncaster, to name but a few.

They were all eager to find out as much about the two strangers that had been caught in the net, so Tash explained to them about the magic, time travelling suitcase and told the assembled audience where they had come from and that they were here looking for some fun and an adventure to remember.

The men listened in wonder and amazement and when Little John confirmed they had beaten him in a duel on the log, disbelieving gasps went round the group quicker than a Mexican wave at a football match, and they all showed Fluke and Tash a great deal of respect from then on.

'So adventure is what you're both after then is it?' queried Robin. 'Well you've certainly come to the right place for adventure, what says you all?' A big hearty roar was given off by the assembled crowd.

Tash asked Robin if the trap always worked as well as this one had.

'Yes Tash, very rarely fails, let me tell you! We normally use it to capture passing rich folk and distribute their wealth to local poor families who need it most. Hopefully the occasional wandering soldier from Nottingham Castle that dares pass through here will also get caught, but unfortunately for you, Fluke here tripped the wire!'

'Well,' said Tash, 'personally I think we were lucky to be trapped or else we might never have met you all!'

Back to camp

The net was reset by Robin and his band of merry men. The leaves were carefully placed over the trip wire, with Tash gleefully helping to arrange and spread them out, providing all the benefit of her expertise in such matters, well she had years of experience where leaves were concerned!

The net was hidden neatly, in the hope that the next folk caught might have enough money for Robin to donate to the poor village people.

'It's only fair really,' explained Robin, 'us common folk, farmers, land workers and the like have been taxed so much we have nothing left. No money, no belongings, it's all been taken by the Sheriff and his greedy tax collectors. All we're doing is giving back to the villager's money that's really theirs in the first place – stealing from the rich and giving it back to the poor.'

Tash thought it sounded a bit like modern day; Dad was always going on about taxes being too high, some things never change no matter what century you live in!

'Back to camp!' ordered Robin, and off they went, Robin and Little John in the lead with Tash in the middle of them chattering away, whilst Fluke was bringing up the rear, walking very, very slowly, watching every step and never taking his eyes off the ground, just in case of another trap. Being caught and suspended upside down once a day was more than enough, thank you very much.

They made good timing, and within an hour or so they entered the outer fringes of the largest camp the pair had ever seen.

'Well Tash,' gasped Fluke, looking all round, 'it certainly beats our little camp in the garden back home.'

Tash was in agreement and was amazed at not only the size and complexity of the place but also how well everything was hidden. Small wooden dwellings that looked like Dad's garden shed at home, only in better condition, were dotted here there. They looked like store rooms carrying supplies of tools, cooking equipment, food and weapons.

Mighty oak trees were everywhere, rope ladders dangling down from the upper reaches and disappearing into the upper reaches of the tree canopy. Rope bridges joined tree-houses together. It was like having a small village of dwellings up in the treetops. There was one oak tree that towered over all the others, dominating the skyline. 'That must be the Major Oak,' Tash said to Fluke.

Something smells good

Campfires were plentiful, with pots and pans suspended over the burning fires, all of which were being looked after carefully by more of the merry men, all seemed pleased to see the return of their master.

One man shouted to Robin: 'Had a successful morning Master Robin?' eyeing up Fluke and Tash with suspicion. The men were always wary of strangers but once newcomers were accepted into the group they were all friends for life.

Robin introduced Fluke and Tash and the residents of the camp visibly relaxed; if Master Robin was happy to bring strangers into the camp it was OK with them.

Fluke's sensitive nose started to twitch as wonderful cooking aromas wafted around the camp; something smelt delicious and he made his way over to one of the bubbling pots and peered inside.

'What's cooking?' Fluke asked the man tending the pot, saliva dripping from his mouth.

'I take it you're hungry?' smiled the cook.

'He's always hungry,' laughed Tash.

Robin agreed it must be dinner time and made everybody find a place to sit and rest whilst dinner was served.

'How do you know what time it is?' asked Fluke, 'I can't see a watch or clock anywhere.'

Tash shook her head. 'Clocks haven't been invented yet Fluke. They use the position of the sun to tell the time. The sun moves around during the day, rising in the East and setting in the West. We have a sundial back home in the garden which helps tell the time.'

'Well that's one way,' agreed Robin. 'But I prefer to use my stomach! If I'm hungry it's either breakfast, lunch or dinner time, and since we've already had breakfast and lunch it must be dinner time,' joked Robin, who by instinct really knew the time was but was having a joke at the expense of Fluke.

The whole camp ate well, starting off with a hearty broth of meat and vegetables called pottage, and fresh bread made by the camp cook to soak up the lovely gravy juices.

Fluke noticed the pottage was the cause of the wonderful smell from the bubbling pot that had caused his nostrils to quiver earlier. It tasted as good as it smelled!

The soup was followed by a pig roast that had been cooking slowly for a few hours over a fire on a spit being turned by one of the camp cooks to ensure the meat was cooked to perfection.

Dessert was a platter of seasonal fresh fruit consisting of wild berries and apples that had been handpicked that morning. Both Fluke and Tash sat back on the log around the campfire, bellies full to bursting, and listened to everyone recounting what had happened during the day.

Each person's story was of their day's activity from hunting for food, setting traps, or spying on their enemies at Nottingham Castle. Gathering information from the Castle was an important job, crucial to Robin and his band of men enabling them to stay one step ahead of the Sheriff, who would stop at nothing to try and catch Robin Hood.

Wood was added to the campfire and everybody moved a little closer to feel the benefits of the extra heat. *No warm radiators or gas fires here in the forest*, thought Tash.

Night-time was fast approaching, and the whole camp was lit by the flickering flames from the fire.

Soon it was Fluke and Tash's turn to tell their story. They began by telling everybody about their magic suitcase, their journey so far to reach the camp and the hope for some big adventure before they had to return home.

Tash noticed Robin taking particular interest when she mentioned the suitcase, and after they finished their tale Robin beckoned Fluke and Tash to sit either side of him.

'Tash, Fluke, if what you've said is true, your little suitcase may come in very handy and I may have a huge favour to ask of you both.'

Fluke's and Tash's ears pricked up.

'Ask away Master Robin, if we can be of assistance we'll help in any way we can,' they confirmed in unison.

Robin was quiet for a while, staring into the fire obviously in deep thought, when he suddenly put his arms around Fluke and Tash.

'What I have to ask of you both could get you into trouble, so think very carefully before you give me your answer,' said Robin, who went quiet again, staring into the fire. A log crackled and popped, waking Robin from his trance and he continued.

'I need to get into Nottingham Castle to rescue a lovely lady called Marion, the prettiest lady for miles around. We were due to be married before she was kidnapped by the Sheriff. He thinks he can win her love himself and intends to force the poor girl to marry him instead of me, but until

Marion agrees to his demands, she's been locked up in that Castle.'

'Anything we can do to help rescue the poor girl we will!' confirmed Tash with a look of determination on her face.

'And we can't wait to be invited to your wedding,' added Fluke. 'We've never been invited to a wedding before,' he continued, thinking ahead to the wedding feast.

'Enough talking for tonight,' said Robin with a grin on his face, 'there's a lot of planning to be done, and the hard work starts tomorrow, but for the rest of tonight let the entertainment commence!' At a clap of his hands a few of the men took out their musical instruments: flutes made from wood with holes fashioned in the top, pan pipes and a lute, a string instrument with a long neck, and a rounded body with a flat front, rather like half an egg in shape.

The music produced by these instruments was wonderful. Sounds reverberated around the forest, bouncing back off the trees, and for the rest of the evening the night air was filled with the sounds of laughter and singing, with people dancing to the rhythm of the music. *A proper medieval disco,* thought Tash. Everybody around the campfire joined in the singing, with Friar Tuck leading the way with his powerful voice, and even Fluke nearly sounded in tune this time.

The Nummers

The morning sun shone brightly through the treetops. The camp was a hive of activity: people scurrying around looking busy, everybody had a job to do and a place to be, whether it was starting the campfire, cooking breakfast or generally tidying up.

Fluke and Tash were the last two to wake. The excitement of the previous day, plenty of fresh air, and combined with plenty of late night singing and dancing around the campfire had worn them out and they had slept really well.

Fluke was rudely woken up, not by any of the camp members, and not by Tash either, but by several Nummers prodding and poking him to move. In the dark, he had managed to make his bed right next to a small tree stump which he was using as a pillow and he was lying right across their doorway, blocking their way in and out.

Bleary eyed, Fluke took a minute to focus and clear his brain, 'Tash,' he whispered, 'look, I've got some of your little friends the Nummers all around me!'

Tash looked over and saw about dozen of the little people desperately trying to wake Fluke and move him out of the way. They were using small sticks, failing miserably to lever his body out of the way, jumping up and down on his belly like a trampoline to wake him – anything and everything to shift him and clear the way so they could get into their home.

'Morning!' a tired and still half asleep Tash yawned, stretching her legs and paws to get the stiffness out of her limbs. She leaned in closer to the head Nummer and apologised. 'Morning Nummers! Spotty will move out of your way and sorry for blocking the entrance!'

The lead Nummer explained they had been out all night, gathering food and provisions and generally doing Nummer like things and now just wanted to get indoors.

Fluke sat up, careful not to harm any of his small new friends and watched as a long line of Nummers disappeared through the door of their tree stump.

'Well I didn't know they had Nummers this far back in history,' Fluke yawned, clearly still tired from the night before.

'They've been around for thousands of years,' explained Tash, 'it's just that they keep themselves to themselves and humans haven't really noticed they exist.'

'Why do they have the long nose pointing upwards above their heads?' asked Fluke.

'So they can breathe easier,' replied Tash. 'Notice how small they are? Because they live underground amongst the tree roots, scampering around on the floor amongst the leaves, sticks and stones, the long nose is designed to poke up through all these leaves helping them breathe. Trust me, having a big pile of leaves on top of you is not easy!' she sighed, slightly envious of the Nummers life style.

The pair rose from their comfortable beds and made themselves useful by cleaning up their part of the camp. Wonderful aromas of cooking reached Fluke's nostrils, which started to twitch and his mouth started to water at the prospect of a big, tasty breakfast, his morning experience with the Nummers quickly forgotten as he wondered what was on the menu.

Breakfast was served, and eaten heartily by the men around the campfire.

Fluke was on washing-up duty; he went with a couple of the men down to the stream armed with pots, pans and all the utensils that had been used to make breakfast. He got stuck into his cleaning duties with such enthusiasm he almost forgot about his fear of water.

Let the training commence

With breakfast finished, the washing-up was done and the camp tidied. Time flew by so fast it was now mid-morning and Fluke, Tash and several of Robin's men including Little John were assembled at the base of the Major Oak, which they also called their council tree. They formed a semi-circle around Robin who stood with an array of equipment at his feet.

'Fluke, Tash, if you would kindly step up to the front please,' asked Robin who had picked up a huge bow and arrow set. The bow was over six feet in length, which was taller than Fluke and completely dwarfed Tash. Robin held the bow in one hand with perfect ease and waited for the pair to join him. The rest of the gang already had their own bows, all of different sizes and weights, perfectly hand crafted to suit each of them. Fluke was first to move and joined Robin, eyeing the large bow in awe, Tash closely followed.

'Big, isn't it!' Fluke turned to Tash, looking her up and down, 'it's over twice as tall as you are' he carried on whispering, 'even the arrows are taller than you, Tash,' he chuckled.

'This as you may know is our favoured weapon,' said Robin glancing at the pair to see if they were listening. 'It's the famous English longbow, used in combat by the few who are skilled enough, and feared by many on the receiving end of its power.'

Robin continued with the lecture. 'The arrows from this bow can penetrate the armour plating and chain mail worn by the soldiers of the Sheriff's army and have caused many an enemy to turn tail and flee.'

Next Robin plucked up a much smaller bow, causing Fluke to nudge Tash. 'Hey Tash, they got one in your size!' he chuckled.

'This smaller bow,' carried on Robin, trying to ignore Fluke's interruption, 'is mainly used for hunting deer and pigs for the dinner table.' This news caused Fluke to stop his talking and pay attention.

'Oh, I thought the mention of food would shut you up,' laughed Tash. 'Master Robin sir,' Tash raised a paw to ask a question 'how are the bows made?'

'Good question Tash,' said Robin. He turned to his men and asked if someone would provide an answer.

'Well,' said Little John, 'they're hand crafted, each bow made to fit the person depending on his or her height. We prefer using wood that is taken from the yew tree. The timber is cut and shaped to the right size and eventually protected by a waxy resin. The bow string is made from hemp fibre which has been soaked in glue and then fitted nice and tight to the treated timber.'

An array of other weapons such as swords, and the famous wooden staff with which both Fluke and Tash were familiar, were being demonstrated by the men, all of them eager to impress both Fluke and Tash, but also their master Robin who watched on with an educated eye, passing on comments, praise and words of encouragement where he saw fit.

When it came to the turn of the wooden staff, Little John looked at Tash and with a slightly embarrassed look on his face said: 'I don't really need to show you two how to use these wooden staffs now do I, as you both already taught me a lesson on how to use these earlier on the log'

'Beginners luck,' said Tash rather bashfully, fully aware that Little John had never before been beaten in this form of combat. A ripple of laughter went round the assembled men; word had spread that the two newcomers had beaten Little John, and a new-found respect had been shown to both Fluke and Tash.

It was a master class. The education went on for most of the afternoon, the lesson was just like being in school but without the use of desks, notepads and computers, much more interesting, and no stuffy classrooms or boring lectures.

'Now that you're familiar with some of our weapons, it's your turn to have a go,' said Robin. 'Little John,' Robin continued, and turned to his right hand man as he did on so many occasions, a giant of a fellow with an equally large reputation for skilful combat techniques, 'please demonstrate the power of the archer!'

The archery contest

Little John picked up his own huge bow and showed Fluke and Tash how to stand, and where they should hold the bow. 'See that target over there?' Little John pointed out a tree several hundred feet away.

Fluke squinted and could just about make out the target nestled between several trees and smaller bushes. The tree had a series of circles scratched into the bark, one large outer circle with several smaller circles inside each other, the smallest barely visible from this distance.

Little John took careful aim, his body as still as a statue, arm drawn back as far as the bow string would allow, and let fly with his arrow which whistled through the air with such speed, power and precision it had stuck in the tree before Fluke and Tash had time to blink.

The assembled men cheered and applauded Little John's effort as his arrow had struck dead centre of the smallest circle.

'Crikey! That was some shot,' Tash whispered to Fluke out of the corner of her mouth. 'Lucky for us they're on our side!'

'Do you want us to get your arrow back?' said Fluke, eager to help.

'Leave it where it is,' said Robin, trading places with Little John and assuming the same stance. His arrow was taken from the bag of arrows strapped to his back over his shoulder and he loaded it into his bow in one swift easy motion. Speed was of the essence in battle.

A hush had fallen over the assembled men as Robin drew back his bow string and let fly: the arrow seemed to travel even faster than Little John's had. An almighty roar went up as Robin's arrow not only hit the same tree but split Little John's arrow neatly in two.

Fluke and Tash were speechless: that shot was near on impossible, but obviously to Robin's men this was a common occurrence – they were all good shots, but Robin really was a master showman when it came to archery competitions.

Next up was Tash. She unstrapped her little bow from her shoulder and was guided into position by Little John, with Robin again keeping a watchful eye. She loaded her arrow into the bow, and pulled on the bow string with all her strength and released her arrow which sailed away through the trees, falling short of the intended target by a few feet.

Several more attempts were made by Tash, each effort getting closer until eventually she reached the tree and her arrow was stuck firmly in the bark, not quite in the circles, but at least she had hit the right tree. Her arrow bag was now empty, so Fluke eagerly exchanged places.

'Not bad for your first few efforts,' said Robin, who along with Little John and the rest of the men applauded Tash as she swapped places with Fluke, who tried to appear confident but was a bag of nerves, legs trembling as he strode up and assumed his position.

A respectful silence fell over the gathered crowd as they waited eagerly to see what Fluke could offer. He reached behind him and took out his first arrow, which he tried to fit into the bow the wrong way round, the sharp tip of the arrow was pointing towards his face.

Little John coughed and Fluke turned the arrow round to face the right way, felt his face flush with embarrassment and tried to cover his mistake with a joke. 'Always comes in handy if the enemy are sneaking up behind you!' he quipped.

He calmed his nerves as best he could, drew back the bow string, which unfortunately slipped through his sweaty paws too early and released the arrow before he had taken proper aim.

The arrow flew sideways, skidded along the ground and went between Tash's legs and struck deep into a tree stump just behind Tash, nearly wiping out a couple of Nummers who were watching the action from their open doorway.

They looked on in horror as the arrow whizzed towards them, and stuck firmly into their front door. They didn't hang around much longer and with much fist waving retreated to the safety of their house; the door slammed shut with the arrow still firmly embedded in their wooden door.

Tash retrieved the wayward arrow and handed it back to Fluke who tried again, this time taking a deep breath before he took careful aim.

Just before he was going to let loose his second shot, a feather from a roosting bird in the trees above fluttered down and wafted gracefully in front of Fluke's face. The feather came to rest on the tip of Fluke's nose, which tickled and caused his nose to twitch. The inevitable sneeze that followed was a split second before he released the arrow. The sneeze echoed around the forest, the tip of his arrow pointed skyward and everybody in the crowd ducked and took cover just in case it headed their way.

Once released, the arrow flew skywards, through the tree branches, causing a couple of the roosting birds to fly off to find a safer place to build a nest, ricocheted off a couple of large tree branches, and ended up heading towards the original target.

Fluke had fired with his eyes shut (you can't sneeze and keep your eyes open). He opened them and looked around. Everybody was gathered around the target tree. He made his way over and pushed to the front to see what the murmurings were about.

Not only had the arrow found the right tree, but it had split neatly down the middle both existing arrows fired by Little John and Robin Hood.

'Well what a lucky shot!' said Tash with a grin, 'no wonder they call you Fluke!'

The whole assembly of archers laughed and congratulated Fluke on beating their Master Robin. 'Not bad, Fluke,' said Robin who was also laughing and patted Fluke on the back. 'We all need a bit of luck in life!'

Training was over for the day and two more days of intensive training followed, then all the weapons were thoroughly cleaned and carefully stored away. Fluke and Tash had proved themselves capable of handling all the weapons that had been demonstrated and just as well because the next time they would be used wouldn't be a training exercise, they would be used for real in the attempted release of Maid Marion from the clutches of the evil Sheriff at Nottingham Castle.

Everybody went off to do their chores and ready the camp for tonight's feast and more importantly this evening Robin would hold a council of war, the final meeting before tomorrow's dangerous trip to the Castle. Everybody knew tonight's dinner could be their last together as a group: attacking the Castle would be dangerous, and they might not all return to camp; but everybody would take this risk for their beloved Master Robin.

Return of the magic suitcase

Whilst everybody else in camp had been preparing for dinner and tonight's meeting, Tash had taken Robin to their original landing spot (well crash landing spot!)

Tash expertly guided the way, and after spending a couple of minutes trying to locate the exact hiding place, Tash, with a grin on her face, leapt into a big mound of leaves and dragged the battered old suitcase out of its hiding place. After dusting twigs, leaves and lichen off the suitcase, she turned to Robin and proudly said: 'There she is Master Robin sir, your transport to the Castle awaits!'

Could this battered old case really be as magical as Tash has made out? Robin thought to himself. And could this beat up old relic of a case *really get us inside the Castle?* He carried on with his thoughts but was interrupted by Tash.

'Let me show you how it works,' said Tash, enjoying the fact that for a change it was her turn to be teacher with Robin as the pupil.

She started to explain the workings of the suitcase to Robin, who was eagerly listening and taking in the information, 'you set the dials here,' she said pointing to the combination locks. 'One set of dials is for the date and the other set of dials is used to set the co-ordinates of the destination you want to travel to,' she purred.

She opened the case, and reached inside for the little booklet that had been in the case lining all those years.

This book was the one they could never dare to lose. It contained all sorts of vital information on travel destinations, time spans, events in history and co-ordinates, all written down in an old gothic style of print on really old looking parchment paper. Without it they would be marooned here for ever and would never be able to use the case to travel ever again. Carefully flicking through the old antique book, Tash eventually found the page she was looking for. Studying the contents of the book carefully, she reached over to set the dials.

Having double checked that the settings had been adjusted correctly, and happy that everything was in order, she carefully placed the battered old book back inside the case and shut the lid.

'We don't need to alter the time and date as we're not going forwards or back in history,' she confirmed. 'We only need to change the location settings,' she said to Robin as she climbed on board the suitcase, and instructed Robin to do the same. 'You sit on the opposite side facing me and hang on!'

'I take it we're not walking back to camp then?' questioned Robin whilst attempting to straddle the suitcase with as much dignity as possible.

Balanced on top of the suitcase and facing Tash, his knuckles turned white as Tash casually remarked *Prepare for lift off!,* and turned the handle three times.

The case started to spin, the wind picked up and whirled around them, and Robin, who'd never flown before, looked down in awe as the ground disappeared beneath him to be replaced by fluffy white clouds looking suspiciously like a great herd of big woolly sheep.

Within a few seconds the case landed, slap bang in the middle of the assembled group of men, all waiting for their master's return. They scattered in different directions as the case made an untidy landing, coming to rest against the base of the council tree.

Another crash landing

'The landing's getting better,' said Tash picking herself up and rubbing her head.

Robin also picked himself up off the floor, dusted himself down, and turned to his men, who slowly re-grouped and gathered around their master, all looking in awe at the old suitcase.

They had all heard about this magical suitcase, but nobody knew exactly what to expect.

A hush had fallen over the camp, with people speaking in low whispering tones to each other. Even the birds in the trees and small animals that inhabited the bushes, shrubs and undergrowth that normally produced the sounds of the forest had fallen quiet, waiting for Robin to speak.

Grinning from ear to ear, Robin exclaimed. 'This magic suitcase,' Robin pointed to the battered old case, currently propped upside down against the base of the tree, 'could be the answer to our prayers! It's amazing! It took us two hours of hiking to locate the hiding place, through the forest and over rivers and streams, but it only took us a matter of seconds to return here!'

The noise levels rose from his men, as questions aimed at Robin were being asked all at once. *How does it fly, how does it work, is it dangerous, how fast can it go?*

Robin raised a hand to still the crowd. 'Enough questions for now, we must eat and gather round after dinner to discuss our plans for tomorrow – it's going to be a long day and we need to be ready.' Everybody agreed and wandered off back to be with colleagues for dinner.

Council of war

Dinner had been a quiet affair, and nerves were getting to everybody.

Tash's stomach was churning like a tumble dryer, and Fluke had been silent whilst he picked at his dinner, even leaving some bits on his plate which was a first for him!

Robin stood, and the murmurings around the camp stopped completely. He had one foot rested on the suitcase.

'As I'm sure you're aware, this mode of transport' Robin pointed to the suitcase now taking pride of place in the centre of the camp, ' will in some way be used in our efforts to free Marion tomorrow. After witnessing the power of the case, I wanted to keep the number of us involved to the bare minimum, and had hoped to be able to fly directly into Marion's room and whisk her away to safety before any of the guards realised what was happening.'

The crowd started to murmur. 'But Master,' Little John said with obvious disappointment, 'we want to be with you and teach the Sheriff and his soldiers a lesson.' Everyone to a man rose and agreed wholeheartedly with Little John, 'Aye Master we all agree, you cannot do this alone,' they chorused together.

'Settle down,' Robin smiled, proud that his men all wanted to be involved. He calmed the crowd and gestured that they all be seated. 'As it turns out, we cannot adopt this strategy. We have received some inside information that the Sheriff is constantly moving Marion from one locked room to another in order to prevent us from mounting a rescue bid.'

'Who's provided this information?' asked Tash, disappointed that the case might not be as useful as they first hoped.

'The Nummers ...,' Robin indicated with a nod of his head to a group of Nummers Fluke and Tash hadn't noticed 'have infiltrated the Castle for us and told us what's happening,' continued Robin. 'As we don't know which room they're holding Marion in, we're going to have to do this the old fashioned way, checking each room as we go. But the magic suitcase will help somehow.'

'You know about the Nummers?' Fluke and Tash said together, looking at each other in surprise. 'We thought nobody knew they existed except us!' exclaimed Tash pointing at herself and Fluke, who was equally surprised by this turn of events.

'We've know about them for years, they're people of the forest, living in trees and tree stumps similar to us,' said Robin. 'They're our friends and allies,' he continued, each member sat around listening nodded in agreement. 'We help them, and they help us. They can gain access to the Castle completely undetected and pass on valuable information, and as they hate the Sheriff of Nottingham almost as much as we do, they help out whenever they can.'

'So what's the plan then?' asked Fluke. 'Cos I can't wait to get into the Castle,' he said, rubbing his paws together in excitement.

'Steady on Fluke,' warned Robin. 'Don't be too hasty, tomorrow will be dangerous and everybody will have to have their wits about them and be on their toes, or in your case on your paws!' smiled Robin.

'Nottingham Castle is holding its weekly market tomorrow, with a huge number of market traders and visitors turning up from miles around. The large volume of people attending should help us to blend in without being noticed. The Nummers will also be helping us as they'll be in the Castle overnight on a spying mission to provide as much information as possible.'

Robin turned to the Nummers for confirmation, to which they confirmed their people were already in place and raring to go.

'Thank you my friends' he said to the lead Nummer, 'you've been a great help'

'Could we have a stall at the market?' suggested Tash joining the debate.

'It's already been arranged,' Robin confirmed. 'We've borrowed a couple of mobile market stalls and modified them with hidden compartments for storing weapons. They will be wheeled in by hand. We'll set them up early in the morning to get the best spot, ready for when the market opens. Half a dozen of you will help run these stalls and will be responsible for smuggling in the weapons, which of course will be carefully hidden in the secret compartments.'

A show of hands from his assembled men shot in the air, all volunteering to work in the market. 'Not you two' said Robin. 'I need Fluke and Tash to help with the rescue.'

'Good idea that, smuggling in weapons,' agreed Little John, 'I hear the guards on the entrance gate always check and do a body search on people when entering the Castle grounds for dangerous weapons.'

'Yeah, they're pretty thorough these days with searching people, especially as there are plenty of people out there looking to extract revenge on the Sheriff – he seems to have upset an awful lot of people!' said Robin. 'If we can infiltrate the market then we'll have men in place ready for when the action starts.'

'What are we selling on these stalls then?' Friar Tuck asked, 'if its food and drink I would suggest myself and Fluke look after it!' the jolly Friar continued in good humour.

'Clothes' said Robin, giving the Friar a sideways glance, 'as we're travelling to the Castle in disguise, we'll be wearing tatty old clothes and we'll dirty up our faces so nobody can recognise us. I thought it would be an ideal opportunity to change back into our costumes once inside the walls, and as our weapons will be hidden in the stalls, clothes and weapons will be close at hand when we need them.'

'I take it we need to create a diversion for you once we're inside?' asked Little John, ' so you can free Marion?' he continued.

'That's correct, Little John, we'll need some form of diversion, it may be a case of thinking on our feet, making it up as we go along, it just depends on what opportunities for causing a diversion are provided at the time.'

The discussions continued for a while longer. Everybody had an input and a few more ideas were passed back and forth until eventually the meeting was wound up and the whole group of

Robin's men knew what was expected of them in the morning.

Fluke and Tash joined the throng of people that were heading back to camp and bed; every one of the group needed a good night's sleep.

Curled up under his bedding, warm and snug, Fluke turned to Tash and whispered: 'you nervous Tash?'

'A little bit Fluke, just a little bit,' she confirmed, 'I just hope Master Robin's plan works, and our suitcase plays its part.' And with that they both rolled over and fell fast asleep, dreaming of tomorrow's big day.

Off to the Castle

The camp was buzzing and a hive of activity when eventually Fluke and Tash awoke. Nobody seemed to enjoy the luxury of an early morning lay in.

A hasty breakfast was consumed – the normal leisurely breakfast forgotten as everybody cleared up in record time and assembled beneath the Major Oak.

Tash noticed several men were missing and asked Robin where they were.

'Already outside the Castle with the market stalls, waiting for the gates to open so they can start setting up,' Robin explained to Tash. 'They were camped outside along with hordes of other market traders last night, blending in and making new contacts.'

The assembled band of merry men were dressed in tatty old clothes and were anxious to be off.

Tash looked Fluke up and down and nodded with approval. 'You certainly look like a local poor villager with your costume,' she observed, 'although I'm not sure about the red tunic, stands out a bit too much.'

Tash wore similar old rags, but without the red tunic, and they both looked like a couple of paupers that would blend in with the expected large crowd attending the market.

After several more minutes of encouragement and wise words from Robin, they formed into small groups and headed off in various directions, using different routes that would eventually lead them to the Castle.

Robin Hood, Little John and a small handful of his most trusted men including Fluke and Tash, were the last group to leave camp, and the magic suitcase was securely strapped to Little John's back.

'Why are we all travelling in separate groups?' asked Fluke as he strode along next to Little John.

'We can't all arrive at the Castle in one big group Fluke,' Little John replied, 'that would look a bit suspicious and make the guards wary. And if one group of us gets caught then the other groups will still be free to press on with the attack.'

'Makes sense I suppose,' agreed Fluke, 'have to be a bit discreet, hence these tatty old clothes we're wearing. I suppose the Sheriff will be on the look-out for Master Robin as well?'

'Oh, without a doubt, he knows that Robin will attempt to rescue his beloved Marion. It was probably the reason he kidnapped her in the first place, to use her as bait to flush Robin out of his hiding place here in the forest.'

'Feels a bit odd not carrying any weapons,' said Tash joining the conversation.

'Can't be too careful,' chipped in Robin, 'if we get searched and they find we're carrying weapons of any sort, the game will be up before it's even started. But worry not, my little furry friends, all our weapons and change of clothes are carefully stored in the market stalls, and if everything is going according to plan they should already be in the Castle grounds any time now!'

After a couple of hours of walking, Robin confirmed to Fluke and Tash they were nearly at the castle. At the top of the next mound, the party stopped to rest, and they looked down across the valley. In full view was the magnificent, imposing Castle, set in a commanding position on top of a natural hill called Castle Rock. Part of the lower structure was embedded within the sandstone rock; the cliff faces to this part of the Castle were over a hundred feet high and although the building had an imaginative architectural design, the stone walls looked out of place amongst the trees and leaves of the surrounding forest.

There was a steady stream of people shuffling their way slowly into the Castle, over the outer moat and through into the main gatehouse, which from here looked like a long line of ants returning to their nest.

'Business looks good,' confirmed Robin. 'This many people should serve us well, once we're inside we'll blend in perfectly.'

They continued their walk down into the valley, and joined the line of people entering the Castle.

Robin cast an expert eye over the crowd and noticed several of his men, some in groups ahead, and some behind, all blending in perfectly with the throng of people eager to get into the fortress.

The body search

The queue they were in edged ever closer to the main gatehouse, and Fluke could now make out the Sheriff's men guarding the entrance searching people at random. He also noticed a long line of guards above in the battlements looking down on everybody; the view from the top must give them an uninterrupted view for miles around.

Tash tugged on Fluke's tunic sleeve and whispered out of the corner of her mouth: 'Here we go Fluke, no turning back now!' A small group of guards pulled aside some people queuing right next to Tash, who thankfully managed to get through without being stopped.

Fluke wasn't so fortunate. He was pinned up against the castle walls as the guards checked his tunic for concealed weapons or illegal contraband. The stone walls were cold and damp to his touch and Fluke wondered where the large stones came from and who had to drag them up the steep hill to build this massive castle. He just knew in another time and place, and with his bad luck, it would probably be someone like himself that would be given the unenviable task of hard manual labour!

But the guards seemed bored and didn't do a thorough check, just going through the motions; Fluke was one of hundreds they had already searched and eventually they let him re-join the queue.

Little John was approached by some guards, but he gave them a look that had them scurrying away to search somebody else more their own size as none of the guards seemed brave enough to attempt a body search of this man mountain.

Robin, with his tunic hood pulled tight concealing his face, swept past the guards completely un-noticed, and suddenly they were all within the Castle grounds quite undetected.

The sight that stretched out before them was impressive. Market stalls of different shapes, sizes and colours were everywhere, selling everything from cloth to ready-made clothes, and all sorts of leather goods, clay pots for cooking, pots to store things in, and plenty of livestock.

Cattle, pigs and chickens were everywhere, all making a lot of noise. Seasonal fruit and veg stalls were plentiful, and the hot food being cooked over open fires generated wonderful aromas.

Other food stalls were selling items such as warm breads and pies, and some stalls offered for sale a fine selection of exotic herbs and spices originating from all four corners of the globe. The food smells had Fluke's nose quivering in anticipation; his belly was rumbling and his mouth watering. It seemed ages since breakfast.

'I'm just off for a wander around,' Fluke informed Tash, 'just to get my bearings and spend some of the pocket money that Master Robin gave us earlier.'

'Let me guess, Fluke,' Tash purred, 'maybe a spot of lunch?' She indicated with her paw the extravagant line of food stalls.

'Might be,' shrugged Fluke, and strode off around the perimeter, jangling the loose change he had in his pocket, pausing to look at each stall to see who offered the best looking food.

The market stalls

Once inside the inner courtyard, Robin cast his eyes around the many stalls, attempting to get his bearings and trying to gauge the strength and number of guards present. Beyond the market was another guardhouse and a narrower footbridge crossing over another moat and leading into the inner castle, the apartments of the Sheriff and members of the Royal family whenever they came to visit. This surely was where Marion was being held.

He spotted a couple of his men, Much and Alan-a-Dale, busily working one of the clothes stalls they had set up earlier this morning, already in the process of selling a big bundle of cloth to a local woman, who no doubt would be making some clothes for her family.

Robin made his way over and waited patiently behind the lady. Once she had finished her purchase, she tottered off to the next stall in search of another bargain.

As soon as Robin was convinced no one was within earshot, he asked Alan if there was any news from the Nummers, any useful snippets of information that could aid them in the rescue of Marion.

Alan spoke in a hushed voice. 'Well Master, the Nummers have been roaming the Castle all night gathering information, and due to their small size they've gone completely un-noticed and had a free run of the whole castle. They found the room Marion was being held in and, as feared, she's locked up securely in the depths of the castle, in a small cell, secured with a solid oak door, with a couple of guards permanently stationed outside.'

Robin nodded. 'Good work Alan, you too Much, very useful information, and thank the Nummers for me next time you see them.'

Much added: 'They've had a rough count and estimated at least three hundred guards on duty at any one time, with more in reserve if needed. They seem to be rotating the shifts, changing guards every few hours. We seem to have them worried Master,' Much grinned, 'apparently the Nummers have never seen so many guards in one place at any one time'

As soon as anybody passed close by the stall, the three of them took on the role of authentic traders, bartering and haggling over the price of cloth. Robin gained a few more vital bits of information such as the weapons the guards were carrying and the location of their weapon store-room.

Robin looked around the courtyard to find where some of his men had gathered and headed over to pass the information on.

'Well lads, looks like we'll have our hands full,' he told them as they gathered just outside the local ale house, named The Trip to Jerusalem, built into the sandstone walls of the Castle. Several trestle tables were ladened with jugs and tankards of frothy ale being consumed by local traders, eager to quench their thirst after a morning of shouting and hollering selling their products. 'The sheriff has a full complement of soldiers here today and more in reserve if needed,' he continued. 'The number of soldiers on guard certainly makes it more difficult and dangerous for us to get into the inner castle where they're holding Marion.'

Little John, never one to miss the chance of some beer, finished his tankard of ale and wiped the foamy froth from his beard.

'Guess you'll need that distraction now then Master?'

Robin pondered and rolled these thoughts around inside his head like a dice, thinking of a way, anyway, to get deeper inside the Castle where Marion was imprisoned, when suddenly the opportunity was provided, not by Little John, but by an unfortunate Fluke.

The distraction

On his journey around the stalls in an attempt to find something tasty to eat, and to improve his culinary knowledge, Fluke failed to notice he had strayed too close to a tethered bull.

Now Fluke loved animals of all shapes and sizes, but, for some reason, cows and especially bulls both seemed to take an instant dislike to him. He didn't know why, they just didn't like him. On recent country walks out with Dad, venturing across farmer's fields, the cows and bulls all seemed intent on chasing Fluke out of their field.

The loud snort from the tethered beast caught Fluke's attention, and as he approached the bull with caution, he once again found to his dismay the huge beast appeared to take an instant dislike to him.

'Probably nothing personal,' Fluke muttered to himself, not realising that the red tunic he was wearing was teasing the bull to charge.

As he tried to squeeze past, the tethered animal started to bellow and snort, big plumes of steam coming from its large inflated nostrils. The bull was pulling at the rope that held it in place, and Fluke noticed that the ropes didn't appear to be fastened as strongly as he would have liked.

Fluke passed the bull and carried on, wandering around, gazing at all the goods on offer at several of the stalls close by, nervously looking back over his shoulder towards the somewhat angry bull, hoping the animal may calm down.

But no: Fluke's worst fears were realised. With the animal's owner busy in conversation with someone on the next stall, the bull pulled free from his loose restraints, and with Fluke's red flapping tunic dead ahead, the bull charged and made a bee-line towards the now panic stricken Fluke.

In an instant, Fluke turned and took to his paws. He ran as fast as he could away from the charging bull, around the edge of the market, and all the while his red tunic was flapping behind him, egging on the bull even more. The large beast gave chase and thundered on, bellowing in frustration at not being able to catch the teasing piece of red cloth.

In a moment the market was in chaos. Tradesman and shoppers scattered in different directions. The guards didn't know what was happening, whether or not they were under attack from unseen enemies, as in a short space of time the market had gone from relative peace to this scene of uproar and mayhem. The noise levels increased with people screaming, trestle tables being upturned – and communication between the guards was impossible.

A huge grin spread across Robin's face and Little John burst out laughing, 'Good old Fluke,' Little John said between fits of laughter, 'Fluke's provided the answer to our problems, this is the distraction we've been waiting for! I just hope Fluke will be OK!'

'He will be if he can run fast,' said a slightly concerned Tash, and with that they all hurried over to the stall manned by Alan and Much, made a rapid change of clothes into their normal costumes of Lincoln Green, retrieved their hidden weapons, and all without any of the guards noticing. They were too busy trying to make sense of the chaos that was unfolding before them.

Fluke meanwhile wasn't sure where he was headed, anywhere would do that took him further away from the bellowing animal. For its size, the bull seemed remarkably nimble on its four sturdy looking legs and was beginning to make ground on Fluke.

Chaos continued as Fluke completed his opening lap of the perimeter. The bull was still in hot pursuit clattering through stalls and scattering their contents onto the floor, leaving the angry owners cursing and shouting.

'Fluke!' screamed Tash, 'get rid of the red tunic, it's your only hope!'

But Fluke didn't hear a thing. He was in a state of panic, adrenalin coursing through his body at the thought of what would happen if the bull caught him, giving him an extra burst of speed that no energy drink provider could supply, and spurred him on to run even faster.

Knowing he couldn't keep up this pace for much longer, he looked for an escape route, and thankfully he spotted another gateway. He tore over the footbridge that spanned another moat and led to the inner castle, flew through the gatehouse entrance that housed the guardroom, and passed the startled guards with such speed they didn't have time to perform a stop-and-search policy they normally carried out.

As Fluke passed under a wooden beam with two vertical support posts that formed the entrance into the inner courtyard, his red tunic caught on a splinter of wood sticking out from one of the beams. The tunic was ripped from his back, and fell onto the dusty ground.

The angry bull, still in hot pursuit, also steamed past the guards, who sensibly thought it prudent not to attempt the stop-and-search policy in this instance either.

But just then the bull skidded to a stop and proceeded to trample the red rag to oblivion,

scooping up the tattered remains with his horns, flinging the offending material triumphantly into the air. Satisfied the red tunic no longer had any fight left in it, the bull calmed down, and its owner, who had valiantly struggled to keep up with the chase, finally caught up and whispered calming and soothing sounds into the bull's ear, all the anger now dispelled and in a moment the bull was back to its normal benign self.

The inner castle

Whilst the stall holders picked up their items and trestle tables, the remainder of the crowd formed a heaving mass of people and headed towards the inner courtyard, streaming over the footbridge, all eager to see the outcome of the pursuit of Fluke by the bull. It was quite some of the best entertainment they had witnessed in a long time.

The guards were desperately trying to restore order but failing miserably and couldn't contain the sheer volume of people crossing the bridge. Amongst this heaving mass were Tash, Robin Hood, Little John and four others from the band of merry men. It had been agreed the rest of the outlaws would remain outside at the market stalls in case the rescuers needed assistance in getting back out again once they had Marion with them.

They entered the inner courtyard and met up with a breathless Fluke.

'Didn't know you could run so fast,' said Tash.

'Me neither,' panted Fluke, who was glad he was still in one piece.

'Brilliant diversion,' whispered Robin to a proud Fluke.

'Yeah, had it all planned, completely under control,' Fluke agreed jokingly.

With a quick glance around the courtyard, Robin took in the positions of the Royal residence, the Sheriff's living quarters, a chapel, kitchens and a line of barrack buildings that housed the additional guards alongside the armoury, the place where all the weapons and ammunition for the guards were stored.

In pride of place, and located to one side, was the majestic Grand Hall that housed banquets and was used for parties and any Royal functions. It looked like it was being decorated for a major event. An assortment of multi-coloured ribbons and flowers adorned the stone walls outside. It must be something special as no expense seemed to have been spared.

Robin knew that the inner Castle was like a rabbit warren of corridors and rooms; there would be a lot of places to check before they found the room housing his beloved Marion.

He gave quick last minute instructions to his men, and like the well drilled outfit they were, dispersed quietly and efficiently around the outer ring of the courtyard, unseen by the guards who were busy shepherding the crowd. They took up positions beside the now unguarded doors leading to the Royal residence and the Sheriff's living areas.

The guards had left their posts in an attempt to restore order, and had called for urgent reinforcements. As doors flung open, a long line of sleepy-looking guards, most of them still attempting to put on their costumes after being woken at such short notice, filed out from the barrack rooms and headed towards the commotion at the footbridge.

Order was eventually restored at the guardroom entrance: the mass of people were shepherded back over the footbridge and herded back to the main market – but minus one dog, one cat and several outlaws. With the doors all open, Robin and his men gained an easier entrance to the inner castle than they thought could be possible.

The bull was led back to its original stall, with the owner looking sheepish and apologising to the other market traders and offering a helping hand to turn the stalls the right way up, and pick up any of the items that littered the floor.

The search for Marion

With the information provided by the Nummers from their overnight visit, Robin had a rough layout of the Castle's inner rooms. He had mapped out in his mind where they should head first. They made their way quickly and quietly through the cold stone corridors, fully expecting to be confronted by guards at any moment. It was agreed the best option would be to split up: they could cover more ground in a shorter space of time. All the men had their bugle horns, and a hearty blow on the instrument meant trouble and assistance was needed urgently. This system worked well in the forest, time would tell if it worked as well inside the castle walls.

Tash, Fluke and Little John took a different door from Robin and immediately turned left and crept along another long and winding corridor. Where the Castle was dug underground the cold stone walls oozed dampness; even though the day outside was hot and sunny not much sunlight penetrated this far down into the bowels of the castle. Fluke shivered, partly as he found himself without much of the costume he had started the day with and partly down to the shock of his recent chase around the market.

'Which way now, Little John?' whispered Tash as they came to a halt at a junction of two more corridors, both leading deeper into the castle.

Fluke reached into his pocket, found a coin he had meant to spend on the food stall, and flipped it neatly in the air. They all watched the shiny, spinning coin rotate several times before gravity took over and it landed back in Fluke's paw.

'Heads we go left, tails we go right,' said Little John. Fluke removed his paw that had covered the coin, showing the result to his two colleagues. It was heads, and they marched off down the left hand path. Their way was lit by flaming torches that hung on the walls at regular intervals, all evenly spaced, the shimmering light casting large and uneven shadows on the floor and walls, causing a jittery Fluke and Tash to jump out of their skins when confronted by their own shadows.

A couple of minutes passed when Tash, whose eyesight was superb, noticed their friends, a group of Nummers, ahead of them, beckoning them urgently. They joined up and huddled together in discussion with each other.

'Mistress Tash and Masters Fluke and John,' they said, 'you made it into the Castle then?'

'Any news on the whereabouts of Marion?' asked Little John.

'Well we have good news and bad news I'm afraid,' said one of the Nummers.

'OK, good news first then.'

'We've found where the Sheriff is holding Marion.'

'And the bad news?' asked Tash.

'They are in his private quarters, which are heavily guarded I'm afraid. The only way in is to get past several of the guards and then you have to force your way through the heavy, solid oak door, which is securely locked.'

'Lead the way my friends,' commanded Little John. 'We have a date to keep with the Sheriff,' he smirked.

The small, but ever increasing group gathered together and followed the lead Nummer, a date with destiny and the evil Sheriff awaited, a chance to right some of his evil wrongdoings.

As they rounded a long, large curved blind corner, Fluke noticed several shadows headed their way. He pointed this out to Little John with paw signals. Little John stopped everybody from moving forward, raised his finger to his lips in the time honoured signal for everybody to hush, and took out his wooden staff. Tash and Fluke removed their wooden staffs, and as trained, took up their positions, waiting patiently for Little John's next command.

The shadows, caused by a large group of guards, stopped moving. Little John, Fluke, Tash and the Nummers could now hear voices from just around the corner.

'What was all the fuss about upstairs in the market?' said a gruff voice from one of the shadows to his colleagues.

'Dunno, something about a bull chasing someone around the market.'

'Wish we could have seen it, instead of being stuck down here guarding her ladyship for the Sheriff.'

'Tell me about it.' A different voice entered the conversation. 'Nice and sunny outside and we've got guard duty, stuck down here until after the wedding tomorrow.'

Fluke turned to Tash and Little John. 'Wedding?' he whispered, careful not to raise his voice.

'So the devilish Sheriff intends to marry the angelic Marion does he?' said an angry Little John, his fist tightened firmly around his staff, a look of anger spreading across his face. 'I'm sure Master Robin will have something to say on the matter.'

With that, Little John gave the signal, and Fluke, Tash and the Nummers charged, rounded the corner and leapt straight into action.

The startled guards reacted slowly, bemused by a blood curdling battle cry of *Chaaarge!* from Little John and the sight of a cat and dog, a huge bearded man and a small army of little people rounding the long bend and hurtling towards them at full pelt, weapons drawn and ready for action, shouting and hollering. This scenario was the last thing they expected today – nothing of interest ever happened on guard duty down here in the dark depths of the Castle.

The guards had far superior numbers than the small group heading towards them, but by the time they worked out what was happening and had drawn their weapons, Little John had plunged into the heart of the pack of guards, causing confusion and panic.

Fluke, his wooden staff swinging around his head and whooping and hollering like a Red Indian, joined the melee and managed to whack a guard soundly round the head, who promptly fell to the ground and would be seeing stars for a while.

Tash meanwhile, not to be outdone, joined forces with the Nummers as they concentrated their attentions on one hapless guard struggling to come to terms with what he was witnessing.

His sword half drawn from its scabbard, was obviously in two minds whether to stand and fight or turn tail and leg it. He should have done the latter, as a dozen of the Nummers armed with tiny spears and a large length of rope, swarmed up his trouser leg and were all over his body in a matter of seconds. His attention was diverted away from Tash as he wondered what the little people were going to do next, and as he'd never seen people this small before he was more concerned with them than he was with Tash, who managed to whack him on the shins while he was distracted by the Nummers. She then assisted the Nummers with their rope, and before long the guard was tied and trussed up like a Christmas goose, arms and legs tied firmly together behind his back, his mouth gagged and stuffed full of cloth to stop him from calling for aid.

Little John meanwhile had despatched three or four guards in quick succession and causing the remainder to drop their weapons in sheer terror and beat a hasty retreat, heading back down the corridor they had originally came from. They would rather face the wrath of the Sheriff than this bearded giant who fought with the strength of ten men.

Stealth mode went out of the window, there was no point in sneaking around now word was out that the Castle was under attack from within.

Fluke grabbed his bugle, and looked to Little John for confirmation, who promptly nodded.

'Give it a blow, Fluke, we need to warn Master Robin that we've been rumbled, might as well join forces now.'

Fluke puffed his cheeks and raised the bugle to his lips and blew as hard as he could, a deep resounding noise came from the bugle, the sound strangely different from when he heard it in the forest, the sound reverberating back off the stone walls. Nevertheless, his bugle playing had the desired effect, as moments later they heard a reply, from further down the corridor. The two groups headed towards one another, and a couple of corridors and bends later met in a large open space at the foot of a large sweeping stone staircase, which headed upwards to another level.

So Sheriff, we meet at last

The lead Nummer was tugging at Robin Hood's trouser leg, so Robin bent down and scooped up the Nummer and had a conversation face to face.

'We think we've found Marion up the staircase on the upper floors,' the Nummer confirmed. 'Our advance party that searched last night confirmed she was being held in the Sheriff's private chamber which is under heavy guard.'

'Oh and by the way,' interrupted Tash, 'I wouldn't take too long in arranging the rescue if I were you, we've just heard she's being forced into an arranged wedding – the Sheriff intends to marry Marion in the morning!'

Robin first acknowledged the Nummer, and then turned to Fluke, Tash and Little John for confirmation 'In the morning?' he exclaimed, 'doesn't hang around romancing his women does he? Upstairs it is then, let's find the Sheriff's room and gate crash his wedding plans.'

They streamed up the first flight of stairs, Robin and Little John in the lead, closely followed by Fluke, Tash, the Nummers and the rest of Robin's men.

At the top of the grand staircase, the landing opened out into a large cavernous space, with yet another flight of stairs heading upwards, and several doors leading to other rooms. The lighting up here was better than in the basement corridors below; openings in the walls formed arched windows, letting the sunlight stream through, and as they didn't contain any glass, the breeze and sounds from the market wafted in. Fluke stood up on his paws and leant against the stone window sill and peered over the edge, whilst Tash jumped up beside him and balanced expertly on the edge, both peering through the window at the sprawling market below. With a quick scan of the area, they could see some of Robin's men milling around their own market stall still selling cloth, which also contained more weapons for the men still in the market should they need them.

'Are you ready?' whispered Robin his words interrupted Fluke and Tash's people watching.

'Lead the way Master Robin,' answered Tash, as she jumped down from the window and the party headed upwards again.

'More stairs,' muttered Tash to herself remembering the steep stairs at home, 'at least the ones at home had nice soft carpet to walk on!'

As they stormed up the last of the stone steps, a head appeared from above and looked down at them from over the stone bannister, which then vanished as quickly as it had appeared.

Robin, Little John and the rest reached the head of the staircase, weapons drawn and ready for action, when they heard a lot of shouted instructions from the guards desperately trying to gather themselves and make ready to do battle.

'Careful everyone,' Robin issued a warning to his fellow men, 'I think we've found the Sheriff's room!'

These guards were better trained and not taken by surprise like the previous group that Fluke and Tash had despatched a little while ago. Word had obviously got back to the Sheriff, and the warning had gone out to the guards that the castle was under attack, and the Sheriff knew it just had to be Robin Hood.

A hefty oaf wearing a costume of chain mail, a large sword clutched in his meaty fist, was the first to confront Robin. As he ambled over, sword at the ready, Robin confronted his attacker, and after a brief clash of metal against metal the guard went down, wounded and dazed by Robin's ruthless attack.

Tash turned to Fluke. 'Bow and arrows or wooden staff?' she asked.

'Let's try a bit of archery this time,' Fluke said as he fumbled for his equipment slung over his shoulder.

Little John powered his way through more of the guards, staff in one hand and sword in the other: most were left stunned by his strength. Robin and the others were in a heaving throng of men, battling away, steadily moving closer to the room they thought held Marion. Their swords swished as they carved through the air, and the racket they made when they clashed was surprisingly noisy. Fluke spotted a door opening, and a figure stepped through to see what the commotion was.

'Master Robin,' Fluke shouted above the noise of the battle, 'is that the Sheriff?' he pointed to the figure standing in the doorway.

Robin paused from his battle with one of the guards for a brief second and looked in the direction that Fluke was pointing.

'So Sheriff, we meet at last!' A smile spread across Robin's face as his arch enemy, the Sheriff, retreated back to the safety of his room, the heavy wooden door slammed shut.

'We've found the little weasel!' shouted Robin with glee. 'Come on men, let's finish off these guards and get Marion out of here.'

As Fluke and Tash stood side by side, Tash pointed out their intended target, a big brute of a guard who was about to attack Little John from behind.

The intensive training course in archery skills they both received back in the forest was beginning to pay dividends. Bows and arrows at the ready, Fluke made sure he had the arrow facing the right way this time and with their arrows loaded carefully into their bow strings, exactly as they had been taught, they took careful aim and let fly simultaneously. The arrows whistled through the air with such speed and accuracy that they caught the guard unawares and neatly penetrated his chain mail and fabric of his costume, pinning both his arms to the wooden door behind him, rendering him totally useless as he couldn't reach for his sword.

Fluke high fived Tash in congratulation. 'Good shooting Mistress Tash!' said a proud Fluke. 'Likewise Master Fluke, an excellent shot, even Master Robin would be proud of that one,' exclaimed Tash, both clearly enjoying themselves.

Fluke and Tash reloaded and let fly with another volley of arrows, which again successfully found their intended target. A howl of pain came from the hapless guard who was in the line of fire, his costume of chain mail peppered with arrows that made him look like a second hand dartboard.

He dropped his sword and fled to safety – no training manual had prepared him for this. There was no section that he could remember entitled *How to defend yourself from a dog and cat armed with bows and arrows.*

Realisation dawned on the guards that they were losing, and in unison they dropped their weapons, turned tail, and beat a hasty retreat down the stairs, calling for reinforcements.

The remaining guards unconscious on the floor had been disarmed, then expertly bound and tied up by the Nummers with the rope they had brought with them.

Robin glanced around the room staring at the bound and trussed guards, many still unconscious and quickly took stock of the situation. Little John and the rest of the men formed a semi-circle around their master and awaited further instructions.

Who turned the lights out?

'We better move quickly,' said Robin, rubbing his chin in deep thought. 'They'll be back with reinforcements pretty soon, so we better make the most of this opportunity and get inside the Sheriff's room before they return,' he said staring at the solid oak door in frustration, 'anyone got any good ideas?'

Tash stepped up to the front and pointed to Little John's back. 'The suitcase?' she offered in hope.

Robin slapped his forehead in frustration. 'Of course!' he exclaimed. 'What with all the excitement of the past few minutes I forgot we had the ultimate secret weapon.'

Little John smiled sheepishly, 'must admit I forgot as well, some right hand man I've been this afternoon!'

'Nonsense, you've been a hero, as have all of you,' he gazed with pride at his trusty and faithful men, 'I couldn't have pulled this off without any of you'

Fluke and Tash helped relieve Little John of the suitcase and set it down on the ground at Robin's feet.

'Well, now what?' said one of Robin's men. 'In case you hadn't noticed, the door's still locked and the case doesn't look like it would make much of a battering ram.'

Tash laughed. 'Me and Fluke will ride the case – it has to be us, as we're the only two who know how to use it. We'll set the co-ordinates to land on the other side of the door, inside the room, and unlock the door from the inside, letting you all in.'

'Not a bad idea Tash,' said Robin, 'but you're forgetting one thing. The Sheriff is on the other side and he'll be armed and dangerous. I couldn't possibly let you go in alone.'

The Nummers shouted up to Robin, 'we can climb in through the keyhole, we're small enough and there's more than enough of us to cause the Sheriff a problem whilst these two work their magic with the suitcase.'

It was agreed. The Nummers clambered up onto Fluke's back, who just happened to be the ideal height. Fluke's nose was just level with the keyhole, and the small army of Nummers streamed over his back and onto his head, down his nose, and poured through the keyhole. Their little feet marching on the end of Fluke's nose tickled and almost made him sneeze.

Tash meanwhile was busy setting the co-ordinates and once the last of the Nummer's had gone through the keyhole Fluke made his way over to Tash. They both leapt aboard and sat astride the magic suitcase.

With last minute instructions from Robin that they were to get the door open as quickly as possible, Tash turned to Fluke and asked if he was ready. The handle was turned three times and the room started to spin, and within a matter of seconds the case had disappeared from one side of the door and landed they hoped in the room beyond. Robin had his ear to the solid oak door listening, and heard a muffled crashing noise, turning to his men he smiled.

'I think they've landed, and it doesn't sound like Tash's steering has got any better!'

Tash and Fluke had been plunged into darkness: they couldn't even see their paws in front of their faces. Fluke's eye's desperately tried to adjust to the dark, and said 'Who turned the lights out? Tash, I think I've gone blind, I can't see a thing!'

'Me too,' said Tash. 'Where are we?' She was groping around to get her bearings and walked straight into a solid wall.

At this point they both heard a familiar small muffled voice coming from one of the Nummers.

'Well done you two, you've only gone and landed in a wardrobe!'

Sure enough, Fluke reached out with his paws and felt a long line of furry robes, tunics and other clothes, and they had, as the Nummer had kindly pointed out, landed slap bang in the middle of the Sheriff's large wardrobe.

They fumbled in the dark for a handle and flung back the wooden door. Tash and Fluke tumbled out of the wardrobe coming face to face with the Sheriff. But he had already been cornered by the Nummers who were swarming up his legs and busily beginning to tie him up with their incredibly strong ropes.

A look of bewilderment and panic was etched on the Sheriff's face as he couldn't grasp what was happening to him. Firstly he was under attack from an army of little people and now a dog and cat, both fully armed, had leapt out of his wardrobe. He wriggled his legs free of some of the rope and fled his living quarters making good his escape through a secret stone panel built into the wall next to the grand fireplace. The concealed stone panel closing neatly behind him, the only evidence left, was a long trail of the rope the Nummers had nearly managed tied him up with, disappearing under the secret passage door.

Tash heard a polite cough, and they both turned to see, sitting at a dressing room table, the most beautiful lady they had ever seen. Marion rose from her seat and walked over, a confused look on her face.

'I don't know who you are! But thank you for chasing away the Sheriff. How on earth did you manage to get inside the wardrobe?' she questioned.

'Er, sorry my lady,' spluttered Fluke, who could feel himself blush, 'I'm Fluke, and this is Tash, and they are the Nummers. We're all here to rescue you!'

'Yes, sorry about our entrance' said Tash, 'we're here with Master Robin as part of the rescue mission. Master Robin's just outside the door now with Little John.'

'Robin's here?' she said excitedly and rushed over to the locked door, quickly inserted a spare key, flung open the door and fell into the outstretched arms of Robin who was waiting patiently outside.

'Oh Robin, I never thought I'd get to see you again,' she began to sob, tears of joy trickling down her pretty face.

They entered the room, Marion clinging to Robin and not wanting to let go. Robin looked warily around the room for the elusive Sheriff.

'Where's he gone Marion?'

'Through a secret passage over there by the fireplace,' she pointed to the opposite stone wall.

'Oh Robin, he planned to marry me tomorrow, I didn't know what to do, he's horrible and been blackmailing me. He told me if I didn't marry him he would arrest my family and throw away the key and they would never see the light of day again. I couldn't let that happen, I just couldn't!' she cried out in anguish. 'I've tried to escape so many times but he's kept me locked up here in the Castle, making me change rooms so I never knew exactly where I was.'

'Now, now Marion, calm down,' Robin uttered the soothing words, 'we're here to take you home. We'll make sure your family is safe as well, that I promise, but first we have to get you out of here.'

He looked around for inspiration. 'We can fight our way out, but I couldn't risk putting Marion in danger – there must be another way out of this Castle.'

The zip wire

Tash stepped up and tugged on Robin's sleeve. 'Why don't we transport Marion out of here on the magic suitcase? Fluke, you can fly it, you've seen me control it a few times now, and we can use some of the Nummers never-ending rope, climb through the window and down the wall, cats are great at climbing things!'

The Nummers interrupted and suggested as they were high up near the top of the Castle, instead of abseiling down the wall, which Tash could do but everybody else would struggle, why didn't they create a zip wire? The men could use their arrows to fire some rope out of the windows, over the castle walls, and into the edge of the forest just a short distance past the Castle walls.

It was agreed. Not only would they not have to fight their way out of the Castle risking injury, but the men remaining in the market would see Robin use the zip wire and realise he'd escaped. They could then slip out from the market discreetly and head back to camp.

The Nummers provided a huge amount of their fine threaded rope that never seemed in short supply. Robin made sure all the knots were tied firmly, and stood next to Little John, both opting to use their longbows, as they needed both power and accuracy for this next part of the plan.

The Longbow could fire arrows a lot farther than the average bow could. They stood side by side, stretched back their bow strings as far as they could, and let fly. Their arrows arced gracefully through the air, over the Castle walls and embedded themselves firmly in a huge oak tree that sat majestically on the edge of the forest.

Robin looked around the room for something to tie the other end of the rope too. He tied the loose ends around some heavy duty iron hooks fastened securely into the stone walls, pulled the rope as tight as he could and turned to face his colleagues.

'Fluke, Marion, you two go first. I want to make sure you've escaped before we leave, and we'll see you shortly.'

Robin hugged Marion firmly and said they would meet up again in a couple of hours. Tash gave Marion last minute instructions, made sure she was comfortable, and turned to Fluke.

'You know what to do Fluke. Take it nice and steady and try not to crash land it back at the camp!'

'Tash, Master Robin, Little John and the rest of you, please be careful on the zip wire, we've all come too far to have any accidents now!' Fluke said with a look of anguish on his face.

Fluke sat astride the suitcase and faced the beautiful Maid Marion, a truly wonderful lady, who could easily be mistaken for a princess. Not that Fluke had ever met a princess before, but figured if ever he did they would be beautiful just like Marion.

'I've never driven this on my own before,' he apologised in advance, 'I'm normally the passenger and I haven't had any driving lessons what so ever!'

'You'll be fine,' said Marion, leaning in closer and gave Fluke a quick kiss on his forehead, 'just for luck' she continued. Fluke felt his cheeks go cherry red with embarrassment.

With everything set, Fluke carefully checked the co-ordinates, turned the handle three times, and with everybody watching in awe, the case started to spin and then promptly disappeared from sight.

'Wow,' said Robin turning to Tash, 'that is some case you've got there! Are we ready?' he turned to his men.

Everybody nodded in agreement and took their positions next to the window. Tash had rummaged through the Sheriff's clothes and had ripped up one of his heavy duty costumes, tearing the fabric into long strips. She tied one end of the fabric around one wrist, passed the material over the top of the zip wire, and wrapped the other end around the other wrist. She intended using the cloth to prevent her burning her paws going down the zip wire.

Tash stepped up onto the window sill and looked down nervously, the ground seemed an awful long way away. Robin asked if she was ready and then gave her a gentle push. Hanging onto the fabric cloth as if her life depended on it, she sailed down the zip wire, gathering speed with every second. She flew over the market, but most of the people below were oblivious to what was happening just above their heads. She flew over the Castle walls and headed towards the long line of mature oak trees, standing together like sentries on guard duty.

Just before the zip wire came to an end, Tash released her grip on the cloth fabric and dropped the short distance to the floor below, thankfully for a nice soft landing in a big pile of leaves.

Oh, lovely leaves! She thought to herself as she rolled around, and for a brief second she was home in their back garden again.

The sight of the next person hurtling down the zip wire brought Tash back to reality, and she just

managed to get out of the way as he too dropped into the soft cushion of leaves.

One by one they all flew down the zip wire, Robin being the last to arrive and land safely. Little John cut the zip wire.

'Can't have anybody following us down the zip wire can we?' he smiled to Robin.

'I managed to spot some of our men as I flew over the market,' said Robin, 'I gave them a quick warning note from my bugle as I flew overhead causing them to look up, they saw it was me and will no doubt spread the word we've escaped and the rest of men should be here shortly' Robin confirmed.

Sure enough within half an hour the merry men were all together again, a brief exchange of stories passed between them all.

'Let's just hope Fluke and Marion made it back OK,' Robin said as the group headed off back to camp.

A Lincoln green wedding

Robin, Little John, Tash and the rest of the rescue party made it safely back to camp. On route, Robin had stopped off at Marion's house, and explained to her parents that their daughter was now safe from the evil clutches of the Sheriff, and invited the family to join the rest of the commune and live permanently in Sherwood Forest. The best carpenters that Robin had at his disposal improved Robin's current accommodation, he had the luxury of Marion living with him now, and created an extension to the side, an annexe purposely built for Marion's parent's to live in.

Fluke and Tash helped the carpenter construct the new tree-top dwelling. Tash had some limited experience in creating dens, camps and hideaways at home and the carpenter was impressed with some of her suggestions.

On Robin and Marion's first night together in their new home, Robin went down on one knee and proposed to Marion. She gracefully accepted and an immediate wedding was planned for the weekend, two days away.

Preparations for the big day were thorough. The camp was a hive of activity as the whole place was spruced up and decorated. Fluke went off with Little John to gather food for the wedding night banquet, and they came back laden with baskets full of treats. The cooks had prepared a large pig roast, and Fluke helped keep a watchful eye and turned the meat regularly so it didn't burn. Venison was also on the menu along with a special home-made wedding cake that one of the cooks had prepared.

'Tash, Fluke, have you got a minute?' Robin put his arms round the shoulders of the pair as they walked around the edge of the camp. 'It would be an honour and a privilege if you two, along with Little John, would agree to be my best men for the wedding. We've been through so much together in a short space of time, but I feel like we've known each other for ever!'

They enthusiastically agreed, and disappeared off into the woods to write a speech and try to agree on who was going to look after the wedding ring.

The day of the wedding arrived. Friar Tuck was going to carry out the ceremony and was busy sorting out where people were going to sit.

With the magic suitcase being, well, magic, Fluke and Tash put their old dirty laundry inside, left it a couple of seconds and then pulled out a clean and fresh change of clothes, both agreeing they looked smart and it was about time they had a change as the last set had seen some action and were beginning to whiff a bit!

The camp was crowded. People sat watching from makeshift seating, men women and children sat on branches of the trees, and even the Nummers were invited – small families of them sat outside their little tree stump houses. An excited babble of noise spread around the camp, everybody waiting for the ceremony to start.

Two loud and long lasting notes blown from the buglers' horns echoed around the forest. This was the pre-arranged signal that everybody had been waiting for. Every man, woman and child looked around as Marion and Robin made their way to the front and stood before Friar Tuck.

They both wore splendid costumes. Robin looked majestic and Marion didn't want a white wedding – she lived in the forest now and favoured a not so traditional Lincoln green wedding.

Fluke, Tash and Little John stood beside Robin and carried out their tasks to perfection, not one mishap, Fluke didn't lose the ring, the speeches went well and when Friar Tuck turned to Robin and Marion and said: 'I now pronounce you man and wife, you may kiss the bride,' a huge cheer went around the camp, and the celebrations started that would carry on long into the night.

Home time

The next morning everybody had a lie-in; no one was rushing and people sat round enjoying a leisurely breakfast – mainly left-overs from last night's wedding feast. Fluke and Tash sat side by side nibbling at their plates of food, both deep in thought.

'Tash, I've been thinking.'

'Well that makes a change,' laughed Tash.

'No, seriously, Tash, what happens now? I mean we've had a great time and all, made some great friends, rescued Marion, been to a wedding and had a really great adventure.'

'Sounds like great minds think alike, you're the same as me. As much as we love it here, the open forest, nature at your paw tips, fresh air in abundance and wonderful people, I'm really beginning to miss home, little things like a nice comfy sofa to sleep on, watch a bit of television and I'm even missing Mum and Dad!'

'Oh crikey, I forgot about them,' said Fluke. 'They'll be panicking about us two, wondering where we've gone, I mean we've been missing for days. The police will be round, search parties organised, we'll have our pictures plastered on lampposts saying *If you find a missing dog and cat please phone the number below*, and ...'

'Fluke, are you not forgetting something?' Tash interrupted. 'We've got ourselves a time machine!' Tash patted the magic suitcase affectionately. 'They won't even know we've gone. Back home only a couple of minutes will have passed, Dad will still be snoring away and everything will be normal.'

They looked at each other and made a joint decision. It was home time.

Fluke and Tash began packing away their belongings in the suitcase, and noticed Robin carefully watching their every move. He strode over and sat between them.

'Is this what I think it is? You're going home aren't you? You do know that you can stay for as long as you want. Everyone's enjoyed your company, the men will be sad to see you go as they've really taken a shine to the pair of you, and we've all formed a strong friendship. We could always build you your own tree-house if that helps?' Robin added, more in hope than expectation.

'We have to go home,' said Tash sadly. 'We've had a great adventure, and we both want to thank you Master Robin, Little John, Friar Tuck and everybody for the friendship you've shown us, but unfortunately we don't really belong here, our time is in the future, we have our own family and friends to catch up with.'

'We understand, really we do,' said Robin, 'I guess it was always going to be when, rather than if you went back. I mean there really isn't anywhere quite like home.'

'Hey, we could always come back for another adventure,' said Fluke, a smile spreading over his face, 'all we have to do is jump back on the case and we're back here again, plus we've got to tell the Nummers back home we've met their great, great, great grandparents!'

Little John and Friar Tuck joined them, both trying to persuade Fluke and Tash to stay a bit longer, but to no avail; their minds were made up – it was time to go.

Little John carried the suitcase over to a clearing leaving the rest of the camp to themselves. Tash and Fluke had said they didn't want any long goodbyes with the whole camp, so only Robin, Little John and Friar Tuck stood in the clearing whilst Tash set the co-ordinates on the magic suitcase.

Finally happy that everything was OK, they both hopped aboard their magic suitcase and said fond farewells with handshakes all round and lots of hugs and back slapping.

Tash turned the handle three times and the case started to spin and then promptly vanished into thin air. Robin listened for a while, just in case he heard any crashing noises from Tash's steering, but the whole forest was silent; they really had gone home.

Egypt adventure

The case made an unceremonious landing in the spare room, and skidded to a halt against the warm radiator under the window.

As they both stepped off the case, Fluke looked across the room at the red neon glow from the digital clock radio. The time said 12:24, so only two minutes had passed since they left what seemed like days ago.

A familiar sound of Dad's snoring could be heard coming from the bedroom across the landing.

Tash turned to Fluke, smiled and whispered: 'Good to be home!'

They hurriedly got changed, stepped out of the costumes and stored their clothing back in the case. Fluke gave Tash a hand to put the case back in the cupboard, and closed the door quietly.

The last few days had caught up with them. Both feeling exhausted, they made their way across the landing to their own bedroom, jumped up on the comfy sofa and snuggled up next to each other.

The sounds of snoring stopped, and a few seconds later they could both hear creaking floorboards. It was Dad going downstairs for a glass of water. As he came back up the stairs he looked in on Fluke and Tash. 'Alright for some, you two just take it easy, why don't you?' he whispered as he patted and stroked them. 'It must be easy being a pet, nothing to worry about, although you must get bored being cooped up indoors all day with nothing to do'

As Dad went back to bed, Fluke turned to Tash and they both burst out laughing.

'If only they knew what we really get up to!' they both said together.

Fluke yawned and Tash whispered. 'So Fluke, any plans for next weekend? We can always go to the woods, play in the garden, visit the in-laws, or have a boring trip to the shops. Or it's just a suggestion now, but if you fancy something really different, we can always take another trip? How does a visit to ancient Egypt sound? We can see how the pyramids were built, see some ancient mummies, take a boat trip on the river Nile, and there's bound to be lots of hidden treasure! Sounds like it could be the start of another great adventure, unless you've got any better plans!'

Fluke stared at Tash, excitement began to spread at the thought of another trip and he was already making plans in his head.

'Well you can certainly count me in,' said Fluke, and they both dozed off to sleep, dreaming of pyramids, camels, river Nile trips and ancient buried treasure.